Finding His Zen

Tammy Mannersly

Finding His Zen
Copyright © 2020 Tammy Mannersly
All rights reserved.

ISBN: (ebook) 978-1-949931-83-9
(print) 978-1-949931-84-6

Inkspell Publishing
207 Moonglow Circle #101
Murrells Inlet, SC 29576

Edited By Melissa Keir
Cover art By The Write Designer

CHAPTER 1

The fluorescent overhead lighting glistened on the glossy paper as the unruly corners of the new, promotional poster fought to curl inward. Tearing clear tape with her teeth, Zenia Andino fixed the advertisement to the sunflower-yellow wall as she swayed her hips to the energetic beat of motivational music which pounded atmospherically through her gymnasium's main floor. When matched with the whir of stationary bikes and elliptical trainers, the thump of numerous feet on treadmills, and the clink and occasional bang of the weight machines, the din created a unique symphony of noise, a masterpiece she enjoyed daily.

"Is that the guy, Zen?"

The familiar huskiness of her father's voice had her glancing over her shoulder after slapping the final piece of tape in place.

"Of course, that is the guy, Leo. This place is full of different pictures of his face and, look, there is even his name on the sign." Zen's mother—still attractive and slender in her sixties, her accent tinged with her

Mediterranean origins—corrected her husband with a point of her finger.

"Oh, Gabriella," Leo grumbled, wiggling his salt and pepper moustache as he raised an age-creased palm skyward. "I don't know his name. All celebrities look alike anyhow."

"Why would she put up a picture of a different celebrity?" His wife argued. "This is the one they've asked to cut the ribbon with big scissors."

As her mother gestured once more to the poster, Zen cast a look back at the lustrous image. The handsome hunk pictured there—with the million-dollar smile, all dripping wet, a multitude of muscles bunched as he hoisted himself free of the blue lap pool—was coming to the grand re-opening of her family's recently refurbished health and aquatic center in just two days' time.

Butterflies burst to life in Zen's stomach, fluttering around in a nervous tremble of anticipation and excitement.

"His name is Sebastian DuMont, Dad." She drew an invisible line beneath the advert's text. "Elite gold-medalist, four-time Olympian and all-round swimming champion. It wouldn't hurt if you could remember that before he shows up on Saturday."

"You know your father," Gabriella told her daughter. "He remembers every name when it comes to the soccer, but when it's swimming, he's all at sea."

"Bah," Leo exclaimed, waving his hands dismissively.

"He's actually from around here, Daddy," Alexis Andino—baby of the family—appeared at her father's side and slipped an arm affectionately around his brawny bicep. "From our sleepy, little seaside suburb. He lived down the road. We even went to the same kindergarten or at least that's what it says on Wikipedia."

"Yes, but not at the same time, Lexy." Zen glanced at her younger sister, the woman who was her opposite in so many ways. Where Zen was shorter and petite with long

4

dark hair, Lexy was tall and leggy with a choppy bleached bob. Her sister was trendy, wore name-brand clothing, and maintained numerous selfie-laden social media accounts. While Zen preferred the simpler things, was perennially happy, and completely at ease with her natural self and her bold European features. "When Sebastian was five, you were barely a blip in Mum and Dad's thoughts."

"Yeah? Well, Mum was pregnant with you at the time, but that doesn't detract from the fact we still attended the same kindy. Any famous connection is still a *famous* connection, Zen."

Her sister's adamant expression had Zen giggling. "I hope you're not planning on telling him that, Lex. I'm sure you wouldn't be the first to try to claim celebrity status by association."

"Don't be silly. I've got more tact than that." Lexy released her father's arm and strutted over to the poster, nudging Zen out of the way before striking a photograph-ready pose in front of it. "You can't deny I'd be suited to the lifestyle though? Can't you see my picture up on the wall like this? Or on a billboard in the city?"

"Yes. Yes, my baby," Gabriella cuddled her youngest daughter. "I can see it. I've always known you were meant to achieve great things."

"I could imagine *either* of my two beautiful daughters gracing the world in such a way," Leo beamed, offering his eldest a sly wink.

Forever the diplomat of the family, Zen's father had always worked to create equality between his daughters. Even though his wife had a habit of praising the girls' attractiveness, Leo had wanted his children to rely on life-skills beyond their good looks. He had encouraged them to strive for personal goals, creating in them a strength of character and resilience, like the kind his own father had instilled in him. Although Lexy hadn't learned the same dedication and determination her sister had, likely due to her mother's frequent doting, Leo's lessons had helped

Zen flourish and had strengthened their father-daughter bond.

Zen smiled as Lexy pulled free from her mother's embrace to continue posturing for the invisible paparazzi. "Dream big, little sister. I believe if you work hard, you can achieve anything."

"Ugh," her sister groaned. "Celebrities don't *work hard*. They just *are*. Their looks and reputation secure their stardom."

"Alexis," her father reproached gingerly, "I think Zen means earning that reputation can initially take a lot of hard work."

"Not for me, Daddy. I plan on being discovered."

"And why not? Look at my baby." Gabriella grabbed her youngest's chin and twisted it side to side before Lexy batted her hand away. "Is she not gorgeous?" She turned to Zenia, grabbed her hand and dragged her closer. "Are both my babies not the most beautiful girls?"

"Yes, Gabriella," Leo concurred. "We have been blessed with the most wonderful of daughters."

"Okay, parents." Zen briefly hugged her mother before pulling free of the embrace. "Enough soppy compliments for one day. Some of us have to get back to work."

"Dinner is at six, darling," Gabriella reminded her before her youngest daughter stole her attention once again.

Zen was never surprised by her mother's sudden dismissal to focus on the baby of the family. Lexy's demand for attention and reassurance was relentless, and Gabriella enjoyed the opportunity to fawn over at least one of her daughters. Her constant doting on Lexy took some of the pressure off of Zen, letting her concentrate on her own desires instead of only those that aligned with her mother.

When Zen passed her father, he snatched her hand and squeezed it lovingly. "You are the heart of this place," he told her, gesturing around the complex. "I hope this swimmer-man's visit helps *you* achieve your dreams."

"Thanks, Dad." She pecked him on the cheek and then left the three of them, as they continued discussing Lexy's copious star qualities.

She prayed her father was right, and hoped Sebastian DuMont's participation in the grand re-opening activities of the Poseidon's Shore Health Club would give the business a beneficial boost. Although a surge in new memberships had followed their soft opening a month ago, Zen wanted to do everything in her power to ensure the establishment that was bequeathed to her on her grandfather's passing last year surpassed expectations and stood its ground against its modern competitors. Her beloved grandfather had always known her passion for the health and fitness industry matched his own and while he'd included her mother, father and Lexy as minority shareholders on the handover of the original outdated gymnasium, he had left Zen with the majority stake and a substantial amount of savings to complete all her refurbishment plans. He'd shared her dream to turn this magnificent new center—with its state-of-the-art exercise machines, highly-qualified instructors, contemporary classes and indoor and outdoor swimming pools—into one of the most renowned in the area.

As Zen approached the front reception desk, both the sportswear-clad female powerlifter standing behind it and the lazy, sleepy-eyed golden retriever curled up below raised their head and greeted her with a smile.

"Amy." Zen nodded at the woman. "Melrose," she greeted her furry companion with a scratch to the top of his skull. "How's the morning been so far? Any newbies coming through?"

"We had a few before nine. A couple signed up to attend Lenny's yoga class, but not much since." The redhead flicked her braid over her shoulder and gestured to the dog, still panting cheerfully near her feet. "Mel has been doing a great job though, encouraging our members to bring in their canine buddies. I took some people through to the fenced yard, showed them our dog-friendly activities, so I think he might have a few playdates planned in the coming weeks."

"Who's a lucky boy?" Zen bent briefly to rub Mel's silky ears, before looking back at Amy. "So, how are we going with everything for the opening on Saturday—on track?"

"Yep. So far, so good. We've had a call from Channel Seven News confirming their attendance." Amy's eyes twinkled excitedly. "The gym's opening will be a featured story around the country. I know you don't like the limelight, Zen, but you've got to admit that's pretty awesome for business."

"Sure thing, as long as it's Lexy's image flashing on everyone's television screen and not mine."

"I still can't believe you asked her to be the face of the complex. This place is your baby. It should be you who's the star of the segment."

"Definitely not my thing, Ames. Plus, I think you're forgetting that no one outshines Lexy."

"Not even celebrity swim star, Sebastian DuMont?"

"I doubt even him." Zen laughed and strode across to the open doorway leading to the back office, but a final comment from Amy had her pausing before entering.

"I guess not being in the spotlight beside him means you'll have more time to admire his hunky physique from afar?"

"Of course not, Ames. I'll be keeping things strictly professional." She winked playfully before slipping into the back room.

As she did so, the smartphone in the back pocket of her denim shorts chimed, heralding a new email. Tugging the device free, she tapped the screen and read the text bubble.

Morning, Zenia.

Flights are confirmed for midday tomorrow. Accommodation plans have changed. We're no longer booked in the city. Seb and I will be staying in Sandgate at Seb's request. New contact details: Bluewater View Beach House on Flinders Parade.

If you need anything before Saturday, you've got my contact info.
Emmett Hobbs
Talent Agent
The Icon Agency, Sydney

Elation swirled through Zen's veins, a buzz of adrenaline. She grinned and put the phone back in her pocket. Things were coming together as planned and in two days' time, Sebastian DuMont—the gorgeous Adonis and her teenage idol—would be coming to her little town to support her new business. She might have been joking with Amy about her intentions to ogle the swimming superstar, but she couldn't help but be over-the-moon about meeting him in person. She'd dreamed of it ever since she'd tacked a poster of him up on her bedroom wall when she was sixteen.

How many people got to meet and work with their lifelong celebrity crush? It was a literal dream come true and Zen felt blessed by destiny that it was actually going to happen.

CHAPTER 2

The wood-paneled and leather interior of the black limousine smelled refreshingly of new car. Tight seals and closed windows blocked all surrounding noise from the busy highway until only a soothing hum remained, competing solely with the patter of Emmett's thumbs on his mobile phone.

As the driver turned the wheel, veering down an exit lane and around onto another busy roadway, Emmett glanced up from the gadget and looked around. Avoiding his agent's gaze, Sebastian returned his attention to the passing view. He heard the squeak of leather as Emmett shifted closer to the chauffeur from his position opposite Seb in the back seat.

"Are we nearly there?" His smartly dressed companion with a perfectly groomed, graying beard and clear-framed glasses quizzed the burly man behind the wheel. "We left Brisbane airport over half an hour ago. How much further out of the city is this mudhole town?"

"Only another five to ten minutes or so, sir." The driver responded politely, moving nothing but his eyes to glance in the rearview mirror at his two passengers.

"Surely you can occupy yourself with that thing for the

next *five to ten minutes*?" Seb tossed the impish ridicule over his shoulder as he nodded to Emmett's phone.

His agent of fifteen years, who had become more like an older brother, scowled in his direction. "You mock me, Sebastian, but time-management is imperative and what I do on this *thing*"—he held up the phone, waggled it—"continually enhances your career and makes us both lots of money." He lowered the device, and looked back at the screen. "Not that you've had much of a career to speak of lately."

Seb hid a smile. He'd been receiving a lot of these digs lately. "I'm not going to bite, Emmett. You can't convince me."

"But, buddy," his agent pleaded with him. "You're letting yourself, the whole *Sebastian DuMont* brand down. You're barely thirty-four. You've still got one good Olympics in you and so many more championship comps. Why not ride it out a little longer? It would be worth it. You'll see."

"Sure," Seb nodded, his tone full of skepticism. "You're saying this as my friend, right? Not as my agent? And it has absolutely nothing to do with the fact that my contract expires in two months?"

Emmett sighed and adjusted his glasses. "Look, you know the agency wants you to sign on for another three years and I want to do everything I can to support your future endeavors. All you have to do is take the leap and commit. Simply sign the papers and we'll get you back on track. We can calm your media appearances for a bit, organize a new coach and get you back into your rigorous training schedule. Say the word and it's done."

Seb shook his head. "You're still not hearing me, Emmett. I'm ready for a change. I want a new life, a *normal* life. I want to retire from all this, the craziness, the fame, the intense training and exhausting competitions. I don't enjoy it anymore. I want to go out on a high, while I'm still able to win and make myself and my family proud. I don't care about the recognition or the money any longer. I've got enough saved and invested to live a happy, simple life ten times over. I just want to be me, maybe meet someone, start a family, and settle down. It's time."

"Is that why you forced me to agree to this job?" Emmett grumbled, his angular features hardening with his change in mood. "Why you insisted on dragging me to this hick backwater town, promising to fund my minimum commission when you discovered the client could only pay twenty percent of our normal fee?"

"What are you, *hangry* or something?" Seb probed. "Do I have to rifle through my bag to find you a muesli bar?"

Emmett grimaced. "I could use a coffee."

"I'll shout you one when we arrive." Seb patted his friend's shoulder. "You already know my feelings about this, mate. I wanted to come back to the place where my love of swimming began. This gym opening gave me the excuse I needed. Besides, it's great publicity, don't you think?" He nudged Emmett good-humoredly. "Coming back to the town where I spent my early years and first learned to swim—even travelling, attending partially at my own expense—all to support a local health and aquatic center. The media will love it and I know you secretly do, too."

"I'd love it a whole lot more if it culminated in the signing of your new contract," Emmett cut a shrewd look in Seb's direction. "But you're not going to make it easy for me, are you?"

"Gentlemen?" The chauffer interrupted cautiously. When his gaze in the rearview mirror caught their eye, confirming their attention, he continued. "We are here. *This* is Sandgate."

Sebastian stared out the window and took in the faintly familiar landscape. The quaint town center was a cluster of renovated turn-of-the-century buildings, cute stores, practical chamferboard homes, and Queenslander-style houses with sprawling porches. While the beachside suburb had tried to embrace modernity with chain stores, supermarkets and the odd fast food joint, the few new structures didn't ruin the appeal of its charm and slow-paced essence. At the focal point of it all, as though aspiring to small-town perfection, the hub opened up into a curling lagoon, bordered by grassland, and crowned with the most picturesque of gazebos.

After passing the heritage-listed city hall with its four-dial clock tower surveying the community below, the chauffer turned down a residential street lined with a bushy cliffside, only to pop out at the edge of the glistening waters of Moreton Bay.

"Wow, look at that." Seb absorbed the tranquil view, the afternoon sun glittering off the gentle waves, and the green perimeter of parkland reaching out to a wide and populated path with the coastal village beyond visible on the horizon. He watched people as they walked, ran and rode their bikes along the concrete pathway, admired families and friends as they gathered on the lush lawn, beneath the public shelters or around the playgrounds. The area looked idyllic for both locals and holidaymakers alike. But, most of all, it looked like everything he'd been searching for: happy, simple and normal. "How wonderful it must be to live so close to the beach," he pondered aloud.

"Beach?" Emmett disputed with a grunt. "Those are mudflats not sand dunes."

"There are some sandy areas nearby as you follow the coastline," the driver advised, "but this particular section of beach is frequented by dog lovers. When the tide is low, they can walk out for over half a mile."

"Really?" Amazed, Seb looked at the chauffer for confirmation and received it in a bright-eyed nod.

"Many dog walking groups plan outings here," the middle-aged man in the driver's seat continued. "It gives the dogs a safe space to run, interact and cool off. I live over in Bracken Ridge, a couple of suburbs over, and bring my Doberman, Daisy, down here often. She loves it."

Seb met the husky gentleman's cheerful eyes in the rearview mirror. "I'm a dog person at heart, but haven't owned one in years. My lifestyle's been too busy."

Commiseration tweaked the chauffer's gaze. "Well, I'm sure you'll get to greet a few adorable furballs during your visit here, sir."

"Thanks. Let's hope I can make it a long stay then." As Seb's chest lightened at the possibility, he noticed his agent's head rotating side to side, his mouth agape like a clown in a carnival game.

Emmett laughed sharply, somewhat hysterically, when he saw he'd gained his client's attention. "Dogs?" He puffed out the word as though it was absurd. "Seb, you don't need a dog when you have a career that's as important and high-profile as yours. Dogs are time-wasters. They're for people who don't have proper lives." Emmett glanced at the man seated behind the wheel in front of him. "No offence." He didn't wait for a response before he continued. "And what's this about staying longer? We're booked for the week and that's it, Sebastian. After our commitments to that little gym are complete, we're out of here. There's no need to prolong our suffering by staying longer in this mud pit of a town."

Seb watched his agent's frantic display of darting eyes and gesturing hands, and gave him a reassuring pat to the shoulder. "Don't have a nervous breakdown, Emmett. I didn't say I was moving here."

Yet, Seb had thought it, considered it for an instant, maybe more, but wasn't sure if this could be his reality. It would mean many changes and, though he'd wanted that—a change of pace, of lifestyle, of everything—he needed to feel certain before any big decisions were made.

"You better not," Emmett warned him. "I'd travel almost anywhere to work with you, Sebastian, but you'd need to pay me danger money to make regular visits to this sludgy bog."

"You're such a snob," Seb scoffed, finding humor in his friend's disdain. "That is a perfectly decent beach."

"Yeah, for dogs," Emmett interjected.

"How are you any kind of expert to criticize?" Seb tossed the question out there with a point of his hand. "I've only seen you at Bondi once and, even then, you didn't come in the water. I doubt you even like the beach."

"Give the man his prize." Emmett crossed his arms. "I mainly do the water environments for you, Seb. Always have. That's not to say I don't have my standards. Like you said, Bondi Beach is one thing, all golden sand and bright blue waves, but this hovel"—he gestured out the window—"I'll likely need a tetanus shot if I even set foot out there."

"What am I going to do with you? I hope you snap out of this mood once we get you that coffee." As Sebastian shook his head in disbelief, he felt the limousine slow and watched as they turned off Flinders Parade and onto a long private driveway that went the length of the property block.

At the front, across the road from the bay, sat an enormous Queenslander house with a lavish, wraparound porch and butterfly staircase. Over the entrance hung a sign announcing their location: *Welcome to the Bluewater View Beach House.* A small, neat garden with emerald turf and flowering shrubbery adorned the façade, while, the backyard—at least what they could see of it—held a timber deck and tropically landscaped cerulean-blue pool, which sparkled invitingly in the afternoon sunlight. The appearance of the place gave Sebastian a sense of serenity and he experienced yet another notion to stay here longer, maybe even make that move here. There was something about the town, something special. It was more than a holidaymaker's dream. It actually felt like *home*.

"No."

The forceful tone of Emmett's voice dragged Seb's attention back to his sulky friend.

"No, Sebastian." Emmett glowered and shook his index finger commandingly. "I know that look. Don't even think about it. I will not let you move to the smudge-on-the-map town of Sandgate."

CHAPTER 3

A crisp, flawlessly cobalt morning sky boded well for the upcoming occasion. Only a light refreshing breeze stirred the green leaves of the nearby cotton trees, while the warm autumn sun shimmered over the rippling saltwater. Seagulls, pigeons and black-headed ibis lingered on the grassy edges around the health and fitness facility curious about the mounting crowd and colorful marques stocked with information and refreshments. There were still a good forty-five minutes or so until the proposed time of ribbon cutting, but already the gathering throng of public interest suggested the marketing event could be dubbed a success.

Poseidon's Shore Health Club, which had made its new twenty-four-hour access areas available a month prior, had closed completely the night before to ensure preparations could go on without disruption. Even with that extra time, there were some arrangements requiring last-minute focus and, though Zenia and her team had finalized the majority throughout the morning, there were still one or two aspects outstanding.

One in particular—the one Zen had pulled the short straw on—was setting up the silky royal red ribbon along the front entrance. Luckily for her, there were railings on either side of the broad concrete stairway and the adjoining ramp, so she had somewhere to attach each end. Yesterday afternoon, she had tasked a team member with measuring and cutting the ribbon to length, so that the tying would be simpler in the morning. It had been left in a big oval loop on a table at the back of one of the marquees with a bunch of other paraphernalia, including the decoratively large gold scissors.

Hauling the hoop of chunky red ribbon over her shoulder, Zen slipped out the rear of the temporary shelter and wove her way through the congregating crowd. Feeling the silky coil slipping and not wanting the spotless fabric sullied if it fell, she pulled it higher and slid it over her head. The new position created an elegant sash across her body and drew the attention of onlookers all around, encouraging them to part the way enough to clear her path.

Zen grinned to herself as she reached the gym's entryway, feeling somewhat like a beauty queen. Usually the spotlight wasn't for her. She'd never felt comfortable there, which was why she often allowed Lexy to represent the business in all photographs and publicity shots, while she handled any interviews or questions from the masses. Yet, that brief stroll had boosted her already elated spirits. She had to remember, just because she shied away from the limelight and all the flashing cameras, today was also a special day for her, not only for the organization or her family. Today was the culmination of long days, hard work and realized dreams. She'd put so much effort into making Poseidon's Shore Health Club the type of fitness and aquatic facility she'd always envisioned, and she deserved at least a little of the recognition and community love.

As Zen pulled one end of the ribbon free, unwrapping it from around her shoulder, she considered how different things might have been had she decided to step into the spotlight herself today. For one thing, she'd have had the company of a handsome male celebrity, one of her favorite sports icons and an all-round hunk. Her heart leapt at the thought, practicing somersaults in her chest.

With a deep breath, she calmed her jittery nerves and tightened the knot around the railing. Only an hour earlier, she'd received notification from the swim star's agent letting her know that he and Sebastian would be arriving later than originally planned to avoid the crush of the adoring public and desperate paparazzi. By her guess, they were due in the next twenty minutes. Again, her heartbeat picked up its pace at the prospect.

Straightening, Zen stood back to admire her handywork. It looked good—pretty and secure. Now for the other side. She reached for the loop of slippery ribbon atop her shoulder, preparing to flip the coiled sash over her head before moving to the other railing, but was interrupted as her fingers touched the silky fabric.

"Miss Andino? Zenia Andino?"

The masculine voice, somewhat familiar, startled Zen, causing her to turn abruptly without thinking. As she spun, stepping away from the railing, the sash of ribbon acted like a lasso and dragged her backward. She stumbled against the metal rail and the concrete wall behind, fortunately regaining her balance before she fell.

"Sorry," the man continued. "The lady over there"—he pointed behind him—"she told me to look for a petite woman in a black and white dress."

"Yeah. That's me," Zen released her steadying white-knuckled grip on the wall and looked up at him. "Who's asking?"

Even through the basic baseball cap and dark sunglasses disguise, it only took Zenia a second to recognize him. There was no disputing that swimmer's physique, his chiseled jaw or million-dollar smile she'd seen plastered across a hundred magazine covers.

"Sebastian DuMont," she whispered, half in shock at finally being in his presence and partly in awe at how

21

incredibly handsome he was in real life.

"Seb," he shrugged nonchalantly.

She pointed a finger at her chest. "Zen," she told him, mouth still gaping like a goldfish. "How did you make it through the crowd without being mobbed?"

"I snuck around the back of the building. My agent Emmett is fielding questions out the front somewhere." He tossed a thumb over his shoulder and then his sexy smile widened as he assessed her appearance, his gaze moving up, down and back to the sash. "You look like you've been giftwrapped." He laughed. "Or does the sash denote some kind of formal title?"

When he chuckled again, Zen joined him.

"I had been tying the ceremonial ribbon to the entrance," she explained as she tried to remove the silky loop from her shoulder, but found she'd inadvertently tightened some of it around herself. "I'd finished knotting that end before you arrived and…" she tugged at the ribbon, but struggled with the angle and couldn't quite see how she was stuck. "And I was…" she yanked at it, but it wouldn't free itself. "I was…" She sighed and looked up at him.

"Do you need some help?"

His good-humored grin was enough to make her feel weak-kneed.

She nodded helplessly. "Yes, please."

He motioned for her to raise her arms as he neared and she did as instructed. His well-muscled build towered over her, casting shadow as he leaned closer. Zen's heartbeat danced when he reached for her, feeling his fingers gently trailing the ribbon over her shoulder, along her collarbone. She stared at his chest, of what she could see of the sun-kissed skin beneath his navy button-up shirt. The warmth radiating from his body, the fresh, soap-scented smell of him, that kissable neck, jawline, it all had her entranced. She blinked tightly when she felt him pull at the chunky red coil, snapping her thoughts back and she shot her gaze skyward, away from his alluring qualities.

"If I'd known that this was the way I'd meet the swim star I'd admired since I was a teenager, I would've worn some perfume or at least a little more makeup." Her exhale quivered with unease. "I never expected it to be this intimate."

Sebastian chuckled softly and the ribbon's hold around Zen's body loosened. Stepping back, Seb gazed down at her, the emotion in his eyes still hidden behind dark sunglasses.

"You look and smell just fine." He smirked and then lifted the silky loop over her head, freeing her from its constrictive curls. The movement caught a long chocolate strand of her neatly styled hair and he quickly brushed it back into place, stroking his hand over her head and down her neck. "And, the intimacy is nice, too."

The sincerity in his words stole Zen's breath and she stared up at his lips, wondering, waiting, all her nerves tingling.

Seb swallowed and seemed to catch himself as though distracted for an instant and again, he laughed, anxiously this time. "So, I'm a swim star you've admired since your teenage years, huh?" He queried, stepping further back with the change of subject. "Surely, I've got to be your favorite one now? I didn't see any other Olympic swimmers around offering to help you escape from the ribbon-of-death."

Zen grinned at his jest and felt herself settling, her tense limbs relaxing. "I doubt my situation was that dire— it wasn't quite life or death—but your efforts have definitely earned you some favoritism."

"Some?" He feigned disbelief and left her for the other railing, pulling the ribbon taut before bending to attach the free end. "I want to be top of the list. Number one. It's the dream of all sports stars, you know?"

"Sure, I know," she agreed, approaching him with a wary step, then two. "But, the top of *my* list? Why would it matter? You don't even know me?"

With the ribbon tied, he strode back to her, closer this time, invading her personal space. "Maybe I'd like to?" He looked down at her, the sunglasses still shading his eyes. "And"—he tilted his head—"winning is *the* most important thing in sports. I'm expected to be first on everyone's list."

"I thought the most important thing was supposed to be trying your best and having fun?" She forced a challenge into her stare, but only succeeded in making him laugh again.

"It always starts out that way," he told her, a hint of solemnness in his tone. "Okay." He gestured to the length of silky ribbon spread across the entrance. "Ribbon's done. Is there anything further I can save you from?"

"Swim star and hero," she gushed. "How lucky we are to have you here today."

"No problem. I'm being paid for my time," he teased.

"Well, with that in mind, Mr. Celebrity, are you about ready to ditch the disguise?"

Seb touched the tip of the baseball cap as though remembering his hidden appearance. "Actually, it's what I'd originally come to see you about. Is there somewhere I can neaten up before the cameras start clicking?"

Zen giggled. "Sure."

As she turned to lead him away to the back entrance and staff bathroom, she heard a familiar bark and soft fur brushed her lower legs.

"Hey there, furball." Sebastian crouched low to greet the wiggling mass of golden fluff who was wearing a collar, but with no lead attached.

"Melrose," Zen chided, grabbing the purple strap at his neck, securing him in place. "Where's Lexy? Did you get away from her again?"

"He's such a gorgeous boy," Seb told her, though his focus on Mel and the dog's smiling face. "Is he yours?"

"He's pretty much anyone's if there's food or pats involved, but—yes—I own him."

Seb rubbed the scruff around Mel's neck and shoulders. "He's so handsome, so friendly." He glanced up at her, his grin as wide as Mel's. "Maybe he should be included in the photos today, shaking paws with the mayor?"

Zen scrunched her face, puzzled as to whether Seb was joking or not, and then she shrugged. "Well, the gym is dog-friendly, so I guess it couldn't hurt."

Seb beamed and grabbed the canine's chops. "Would you like that? Would you like to have your picture taken?"

Puffing tiredly, Lexy—all dolled up in her sexiest exercise gear—ran up behind him and Mel barked proudly at her.

"Don't bark at me, you little Houdini," she panted. "I've been looking everywhere for you."

"And why's that?" Zen asked, putting her hands on her hips. "I asked you to keep him in the shade on the sidelines until Mum and Dad arrived and then you could hand him on."

"Yeah, and I was doing that." Lexy snapped.

"So, how did he end up off the lead then? Did you take him down to the beach, even though I asked you not to?"

"No." It was an obvious, but indignant lie. Lexy stared at the stranger patting Mel and stuck a thumb in his direction. "Who's the weirdo with the creepy stalker get-up?"

Seb stood to greet her. "Sebastian DuMont." He extended a hand. "Not a stalker, just trying to be incognito."

Lexy's jaw dropped and she shot a look at Zen. "Seriously?"

Zen nodded.

Her younger sister stared hard at the tall, muscular man in front of them, giving him a complete once over. Finally satisfied with his identity, she lunged for him, took his hand in hers and spun them both around to face the crowd.

"You-hoo! It's Sebastian DuMont," she proclaimed to the surrounding public as Zen stretched out to stop her. "He's here."

"Lexy, no!" But, Zen's hold on Mel's collar restricted her reach and, before she could do anything more to stop her sister, Lexy had already linked an arm through Seb's and had dragged him into the sea of people.

CHAPTER 4

The spacious group-workout room with its mirrored wall and durable flooring had transformed into a packed press conference, full of gossip-hungry reporters and intermittent camera flashes. Sunlight streamed in from the wall of windows to the right, while on the opposite beachy blue and yellow wall was a row of collapsible tables, topped with microphones, and framed with banners promoting the new gymnasium and its facilities. Seated there, talking inaudibly amongst themselves as they awaited the beginning of the short conference arranged by Seb's management, were Zen and Lexy Andino.

As midday neared, the heat and humidity encouraged much of the external crowd to seek shelter in the air-conditioned depths of the health and fitness complex. Many had taken advantage of the plastic seating toward the back, behind those already designated for the media. The rumble of murmurings between public and press alike filled the room like rolling waves of sound as they waited, relatively patiently, for their guest of honor to arrive.

As was customary for him, Sebastian had taken his time after the successful ribbon cutting ceremony to sign autographs and take photos with his fans, especially the younger ones. If he was to miss anything from his prosperous swimming career, it'd be his ability to inspire and positively influence those children and young adults to reach their potential in whatever they so desired. Acting as a role model was one of the few aspects of his profession he still looked forward to, so he always made sure to give it the time it deserved.

When Seb finally entered the group fitness room, the Mayor of Sandgate—Terrance Jones—by his side, all attention flicked to them and the cameras blinked a strobe of flashing lights. Zen and Lexy stood, their applause mixing with that of the surrounding masses, giving their guests a hero's welcome.

"What a greeting," exclaimed Mayor Jones, directing the comment solely to Seb. "You can see how privileged we feel as a community to have you visiting us for this special occasion."

Seb nodded affably, but found his focus immediately pulled away, preoccupied with the presence of Zenia Andino at the far end of the tables.

He'd known she was to participate in this media frenzy—being the health center's owner and manager after all. It was just that, he'd felt drawn to her after their first meeting, charmed by Zen's personality, cheekiness, and beauty. He'd caught himself staring throughout the morning, admiring the way she interacted with all the attendees. She showed impeccable patience and friendliness, especially with the children. There was also something extra special about Zen, evident in that smile when she saw her family and playful pooch. It made Seb want to know her better, to understand the way she thought and felt.

His body's physical reactions made it obvious that he desired to touch her, to kiss her. She was a gorgeous woman, the opposite of her sister—natural, where Lexy was "enhanced"—but with the familial attractiveness and a certain exoticness. It had been a long time since Seb's last serious relationship, so he wasn't surprised to feel this way, especially considering his mixed emotions about retirement, but he was concerned about the practically of it all. Was it sensible to start something when he was only supposed to be in town for a week? Zen didn't come across as the type of woman to enter into something so fleeting. It had him distracted, wondering over the possibilities as his hopes and desires churned fervently within him.

"Here, Seb." Lexy ushered him over with a wave. "You're to sit beside me."

When Mayor Jones took a seat on his other side, Seb reluctantly followed Lexy's instructions. As soon as he was seated, Lexy slipped an arm through his.

"This is so exciting," she beamed. "I've never done anything like this before with such a famous celebrity companion." She patted his arm. "Don't worry, I'll be brilliant as always." Lexy batted her lashes at him and then nodded in her sister's direction. "If there are any problems, Zen will handle them."

Seb looked over at Zenia. "Hi," he said and immediately felt ridiculous for not being able to think of something clever.

She smiled at him. "Hello, again."

He stared into her big, dark brown eyes. "Ah…um," he swallowed in an effort to spit out some proper words. "Do you think we could have a chat later?"

She frowned, expression turning curious. "Sure—"

Her whispered voice was abruptly cut off by Lexy's.

"What a great idea! Maybe we could all have coffee together?"

At that moment, Mayor Jones gently touched Seb's shoulder, dragging his attention back to the greying, middle-aged man. "I think it's time we start, Sebastian." He nodded toward the media and audience beyond.

Having tried unsuccessfully to shift his arm free of Lexy's, Seb agreed with a bow of his head and Mayor

Jones stood, switching on the portable microphone in his hand.

"Ladies and gentlemen from the community and the media," the Mayor addressed the room. "We're grateful you can join us today during such a special celebration of health and wellbeing, at the opening of such an impressive fitness and aquatics center which I know will be of essential benefit to all those in our local areas, the tourism industry and the general public."

There was a smattering of applause and he waited for it to subside before he continued.

"Now, we have already made all our formal speeches during the official opening and ribbon cutting, so this press conference is to answer any and all questions you have regarding the complex itself, the facilities here, and our very special guest, Sebastian DuMont."

Mayor Jones directed a hand at Seb and then clapped, starting yet another small round of applause.

"Thank you," the Mayor told the room. "Now, let's get started, shall we?" As he sat, he positioned his microphone back in its short stand.

Seb noticed Zen switch her and Lexy's microphones on and quickly did the same. As members of the audience raised their hands, hopeful to have their questions addressed, television cameramen aimed their recording devices and sound equipment toward the front, and photographers clicked their camera's buttons, blasting them with yet more blinding flashes.

"Yes, you there, the red shirt," Mayor Jones pointed into the crowd at a female reporter toward the front.

As those seated around her looked her way, she accepted his invitation to speak with a nod and then cut her gaze to Sebastian's. "Hi, my question is for Mr. DuMont. Sebastian, you've recently taken a hiatus from your competitive swimming career. Does this indicate you're considering the possibility of retiring or turning your attention to a new focus, such as mentoring or supporting local businesses through endorsements like this one?"

When Seb leaned toward the microphone, his arm still somewhat entwined with Lexy's, he noticed Emmett lingering on the sidelines, watching the interactions of the press conference intently.

"As an aging athlete," Seb answered, plastering a cheerful grin on his face, "the possibility of retirement is often something to consider, but in this case, I believe it's too early to tell." He noticed Emmett's nod of approval, before continuing. "All I can say is that I'm currently enjoying the break from the intense schedule of my usual training regime to support some worthy causes and businesses, like Poseidon's Shore Health Club, which shares in my passion for health, fitness and early learn-to-swim classes."

"Okay. Next question." Mayor Jones glanced around the room as members of the crowd raised their hands. "Yes, you there. Andrew, correct?"

The man in the front row tilted his head in salutation. "Yes. Andrew Harvey. Bayside Herald. Mayor Jones—a question for you. It must be something very special for a small town like Sandgate to have such a world-class complex like this to attract people locally, from surrounding suburbs and tourists alike, and now to have Sebastian DuMont here, participating in the opening, how does that make you feel and how do you think this kind of positive publicity might benefit Sandgate over time?"

Mayor Jones laughed. "Thank you, Andrew. Sneaking in two questions there, I see. Well, firstly, it feels wonderful and I personally feel very privileged to be seated next to one of Australia's top Olympic swimming champions. I'm somewhat starstruck." He winked at the audience, eliciting a murmured chuckle from the crowd. "Mr. DuMont has always been one of my favorite sportsmen and I'm an avid fan."

Realizing this question may have been staged, Seb

beamed his trademark grin and happily played along. "Why thank you, Terry. I'm a big fan of your work in Sandgate also."

Mayor Jones glowed at the compliment and turned back to the local Bayside Herald newspaper reporter. "To answer the second part of your question, Andrew, any promotions advocating Sandgate will always be beneficial to the town and the townsfolk in the future. In this case, with Sebastian's endorsement of this magnificent center and his support throughout opening week, we should expect to see a peak in interest and attendance. As interest grows and more people join the club—we will eventually see a very positive effect on the health and wellbeing of the population in local and neighboring suburbs, which should increase even further over time. We all know the benefits of a good workout, both mentally and physically and Poseidon's Shore has it all—treadmills, spin bikes, free weights, exercise classes and lap pools." He pointed at the crowd, aiming his hand like a fleshy gun. "I know I've got my twenty-four-hour gym pass. I've no doubt you'll be inspired to get yours, too."

Andrew signaled his thanks for the detailed response and the other audience members raised their hands, eagerly awaiting to be chosen.

"Hello, yes. The young blonde woman in the front here." Mayor Jones pointed at the opposite end of the first row.

"Hi. Sara Beechman from the Courier Mail." The stylishly dressed reporter turned her attention to the Andino sisters. "Miss Andino?"

Lexy grinned and tugged on Seb's arm. "Yes."

Sara shook her head. "Sorry. *Zenia* Andino?"

As Zenia gestured for the reporter to continue, the corners of Lexy's broad grin faltered, but she didn't let them fall.

"Zenia, hi. I'm interested to find out what encouraged you to invite Sebastian here to the opening today? Did you know each other before all this or have a common acquaintance?"

"No, nothing like that." Zen chuckled. "My sister likes to remind me that we all went to the same kindergarten, but at different years. I guess"—she looked across at Seb, smiled when she caught his eye—"it might sound a little embarrassing now, but I invited him to come, because he's always been an idol of mine." Zen turned back to the reporter. "I used to have his picture up on my bedroom wall. I admired his determination and commitment, and how he was always so down-to-earth, so easy to relate to. He showed everyone it was possible to achieve their dreams and stay true to themselves, and I was inspired by that."

"It also couldn't hurt that he'd been ranked as one of the world's sexiest athletes, could it?" Sara ushered.

"That was an added bonus." Zen's cheeks blushed lightly.

"On the flipside—Sebastian," the Courier Mail's reporter continued, "what aided your decision to agree to endorse Poseidon's Shore Health Club? It's been previously reported that much of this trip has been funded by you personally. Would you say this might be a labor of love for you then?"

"Very much so, Sara." He flashed his charismatic grin at her and noticed Emmett moving around the room, disappearing somewhere behind him out of eyeshot. "Many years ago, Sandgate used to be my hometown. I learned to swim here and fell in love with the water. I've always felt swimming may be in my blood, but I believe that Sandgate and my first experiences here—with the water, learning stroke, technique—nurtured my natural talent enabling me to become the world champion I am today."

"That's some high praise, Sebastian," Sara noted.

"Look around," he gestured out through the wall of windows at the glorious day outside, the sparkling water and distant horizon beyond. "Don't you think this beautiful town deserves it?"

There was a hushed rumble of agreement from the audience.

"Besides, Sara, I enjoy supporting local businesses where I can. When I heard of Miss Andino's establishment, what her and her family had done to turn her grandfather's original complex into the outstanding fitness facility it is today, I wanted to do my part to promote it and I am very grateful to have been offered the opportunity."

Seb glanced past Lexy to Zen, noticed her heartened smile, the sincere shine in her eyes and had to look away before he fell victim to his own flush of red cheeks.

As though noticing part of the interaction there, the Courier Mail's reporter quickly posed another question. "So, there's not another reason behind the visit then? I mean you and Miss Alexis Andino appear rather close." She gestured at Lexy's arm still linked through his. "Is there something happening between you two?"

Immediately, Seb noticed a shadow looming behind him and hot, minty breath at his ear before his agent closed a hand over the microphone in front of him.

"Go with it, Sebastian," Emmett whispered instructively. "A romantic affair would be good for your image, get you back in the tabloids, and jumpstart your stalled career."

"I'm not interested, Emmett," Seb growled mutedly through a smile of gritted teeth.

"You don't actually have to date her," Emmett told him, his lips stretched with a matching feigned grin. "Just make it appear that way. She's a budding influencer, got a good following. The connection could be very beneficial. You said you wanted to go out on a high."

"Beneficial for whom?" Seb glared at his agent.

"Just think about it," Emmett told him, removing his hand from the microphone and backing away.

"Sebastian?" The young blonde reporter probed.

He looked back at the captive crowd, seeing their hunger for an answer, especially after witnessing such an inaudible, conspicuous exchange between him and his agent. He forced his smile to reach his eyes and laughed, albeit nervously.

"Alexis Andino and I have only just met," he began, but as he opened his mouth to continue, someone toward the back of the crowd interjected.

"Maybe it's love at first sight then?"

There was a tittering through the audience and Seb weakly joined in. He looked at Lexy by his side, saw her almost bursting in anticipation of his answer, hugging his arm tighter and then noticed Zen behind her, brows narrowed in curiosity, surprise in her dark eyes. He had an instant of wishing they'd been seated differently. He doubted he'd have any problem implying something might be blossoming between him and Zenia. But, Lexy? It wasn't right to lie, but years of habit and conditioning had him weakening to Emmett's suggestion.

He turned back to the crowd before him. "Lexy and I…" He wanted to say that they barely knew each other, but something about Emmett's advice niggled at him.

"As Mr. DuMont seems to have become tongue-tied, perhaps we may pass the question to you, Alexis?" The prompt was from another woman, a mature brunette amongst the media at the front.

Seb could feel the buzz of exhilaration tingle through Lexy's arm to his as she wiggled closer to the microphone.

"Sure," she purred, her expression aglow with delight and insinuation. "Sebastian and I might have only met a few hours ago, but I already feel there's a strong connection between us." She cuddled closer to him and he was trapped in her embrace. "We've got so much in common. We're like kindred spirits."

"So, do you think there might be love in the air?" Sara, the reporter from the Courier Mail enquired again.

A wide, ecstatic grin was like a gash across Lexy's face. She gazed up into his eyes, searched them for a second before once again acknowledging the assembly. "When it comes to Seb and me, anything is possible."

At that, the bottom fell out of Seb's stomach and he felt as like he was riding the steep, rushing decent of a rollercoaster dip.

The audience erupted at Lexy's answer, newly galvanized and interested in the possibility of a sexy affair to report on and obsess over. The insinuation of a relationship made Seb feel sick, nausea roiling in his gut. He wanted to correct the mistake, but couldn't see a way out without embarrassing both of them.

Seb felt a pat on his shoulder as the raucous roar of the gathering continued, the audience's arms waving, camera's flashing and he heard Mayor Jones commend him.

"Congratulations," the older man said, his tone genuinely joyous, oblivious to the reality.

With his heart racing, palms sweating, his gut churning on the verge of sickness, Seb cast a look at the one person in the world whose opinion really mattered to him in that instant. He caught Zenia's eye, saw her solemn smile and…seeing that look, her fallen spirt, had pain stabbing into his heart, breaking it a little.

What the hell had he done? What the hell had he agreed to? And what could he do to show Zenia that his true interest lay with her and not her sister?

CHAPTER 5

The liquid skin of the outdoor lap pool rippled as a gentle gust tickled the once smooth surface. Post-dawn sunlight brightened the sky with warm pastel hues, vibrant pinks and oranges, while a new chilliness to the Sunday morning foretold the coming of cooler months. Eventually it'd become too icy to swim outdoors after daybreak and all habitual swimmers and those who were set to join the swim-classes, would be doing their workout along the length of the indoor swimming pool. But, for this morning and the bearable few that followed, Zenia would continue to stroke through her fifty laps in the open-air exercise environment.

Since they'd silently reopened their facilities a month ago, she had gradually been accompanied in her regular training by more and more early risers who enjoyed a good dip. While not all of them completed as many lengths of the pool, most were clearly trained in the sport and displayed good skill. She appreciated their company and their interest in her favorite feature of the fitness center, but was often grateful that each newcomer chose a different section, leaving her with a single lane to herself.

Today was different though, and she'd noticed toward

the end of her set that a bulky male swimmer had splashed distractingly into her lane. Refusing to stop her progress, Zen continued to swim lap after lap. Yet, each time she passed her companion on the opposite side of the lane, she checked through her goggles, trying to distinguish any familiar features of his appearance, though his physique and stroke style had already given her an inkling. When she finally finished, she removed her cap and goggles, and waited at the shallow end for him, catching her breath.

Sleek like a shark, as graceful as a dolphin in his smooth freestyle crawl technique, the male swimmer approached almost silently. Zen moved further to the side of the edge lane as the newcomer's long arms neared and when his fingertips touched the tiles, he curled his legs in and surfaced.

"Morning," he greeted her and then began to remove the reflective, bulbous swimming goggles covering his eyes.

"Sebastian." She tilted her head in his direction and crossed her arms over the wet, black fabric of her swimsuit. "I'm surprised to see you here so early. You're not needed onsite until the workshop at eleven-thirty."

"*Someone* gave me a twenty-four-hour pass, so I thought I'd take advantage of the gym's facilities." He flashed a smile her way. "Well, that and Lexy told me you usually do an early swim session."

She frowned at him. After yesterday's press conference and the revelation regarding a supposed developing relationship between him and her sister, Zen had purposely kept her distance. She might have experienced attraction upon meeting him, thought stupidly that it was they who shared a rather unique connection and let herself fantasize for the teensiest instant of what a romantic relationship between the two of them might look like, but now she knew better. Seb had no interest in her whatsoever and that was okay, she was still grateful for him being in town to support the center's opening.

Nowhere in their contract did it state anything about romantic commitments or expectations. A friendly working relationship was completely reasonable, but it didn't mean she easily accepted the fact he was attracted to her sister—especially when he made it more difficult for her by showing up randomly by her side.

"I thought you and Lexy would have had more interesting things than my exercise routine to chat about during your coffee date." She tossed the comment at him like a loaded grenade, hoping he might burst with an explosion of answers.

Seb put his silicon-swimming cap and goggles on the edge, creating a little puddle on the terracotta tile. "Considering you were the one I actually invited out, but didn't come, I attempted to salvage the situation as best as possible."

"What? By learning my routine?" She scoffed.

He leaned an elbow on the sun-warmed pool perimeter. "Maybe. I mean, I had to do something once I realized you were dodging me, and it's worked, hasn't it?" He winked at her. "I've managed to get a moment alone with you."

Zen shook her head, brows furrowing in bewilderment. "Sorry, but why is it important to you? Only yesterday, you announced to the world you were interested in dating my sister. Surely your priority would be getting a moment alone with her?"

"You were the only one I wanted to spend time with," he told her, his tone deepening with sincerity. "Preferably there'll be *moments* rather than the singular though." He shrugged off his seriousness, becoming chipper once more. "And, we could start by having breakfast together this morning."

Zen puffed out her chest indignantly. "Do I get a decision in the matter or has it been decided for me?"

"Probably a little bit of both."

He smirked at her and that cheeky look had butterflies

coming to life in her stomach.

"You get a decision if it's a yes, but not if it's a no," he told her.

"That's hardly fair."

Seb shrugged. "Neither is having a whole room of reporters think you've got a new love interest simply because the woman beside you says so."

"I didn't hear you denying it." She poked out her chin defiantly. "And *that woman* is my sister and happens to be pretty wonderful, thank you very much. Anyone would be extremely lucky to have her as their partner."

"Are you saying you approve of the relationship then?" Seb's gaze narrowed on hers, staring so intently it made her flinch. "You'd be happy for me to start dating your sister?"

"Don't twist my words," Zen pouted. "I didn't say that."

His sexy smile grew wider. "So, you do care?"

She sighed and looked away from him, out over the shimmering water of the pool. "I don't have a right to care. We don't know each other, Sebastian. We're practically strangers."

"That's why we should get to know each other." He inched closer to her, wading through the cool liquid. "Besides, you've had a picture of me up on your bedroom wall for years, so you already have a head start."

"That's not the same thing," Zen glared at him, "and what makes you think it's still up on my wall?

"Your *bedroom* wall," Seb corrected her. "We have to be specific now."

"Well, I'm getting out now," Zen teased, making her voice high-pitched and swishing her wet hair like a sarcastic teenager.

She turned her back on him and pulled herself up onto the terracotta-tiled edging, then noticed he'd quickly followed suit, bending to scoop up his damp belongings as she did the same to collect hers.

"So, breakfast?" He asked when she glowered over her shoulder at him.

His million-dollar smile was so damn endearing, weakening her knees and her resolve, while his almost entirely naked body—rock hard muscles pumped, glistening wet in the sunshine—gave her immediate brain fog. Zen huffed out her irritation, but conceded with a nod.

"Fine. Breakfast," she agreed.

As she headed off to the showers with Seb stuck to her side, Zen wondered exactly what she'd agreed to. She felt safe at the possibility of eating together, but anything more might tempt her further and he was already on the verge of irresistible. If Zen was certain of anything, it was that when something felt this good, there was definitely going to be trouble.

CHAPTER 6

A light breeze stirred the dark green leaves and teased white tips into the saltwater's gently rolling façade, but it wasn't enough to dissipate the snowballing warmth radiating down. The unencumbered sunlight had really found bite as the hours passed, causing the beachgoers to seek out the relief of the shade. Busy as usual with its breakfast and brunching crowd, the sheltered seaside café—which stretched out with awning and outdoor furniture settings across a popular walkway—provided the necessary reprieve of shadow and coolness.

Zen watched as another couple of sunbathers—lathered in sunscreen, and sporting swimwear and sunglasses—squeezed under the café's awning searching for a free table. The frequent sight had her feeling guilty for having monopolized a prime place for so long, especially since her and Seb had finished eating breakfast hours ago. Yet, the chat had been so engrossing, enlightening and constant as they'd continued to order and consume coffees, cold drinks and cups of tea. She hadn't wanted it to end, but knew as the hours passed that the fitness center's special workshop with Sebastian was bearing down on them. It was well after ten o'clock now and she had already received a couple of curious texts about her whereabouts, which she'd had to address soothingly. It was a shame her and Seb didn't have more free time to spend together.

"You know, you've really surprised me." Zen twirled a teaspoon in her cup of tea.

"Good. I'll add it to my list of skills," he joked. "Surprising—tick."

She giggled and looked up at the reflective covering shielding his eyes. Initially, when it was still early, Seb had enjoyed the freedom of not having to hide his appearance, but as soon as the crowds gathered, he'd opted to slip on the familiar baseball cap and dark sunglasses hoping to remain incognito.

"No. I mean, you surprised me personality-wise," she explained. "I'd always suspected you were a pretty good guy—I've watched my fair share of your interviews—but, before meeting you, I didn't want to assume anything. Then there was that whole fiasco yesterday and"—she waved dismissively—"now, I'm all turned around again."

"Turned around, how?" He gave her that goddamn sexy grin which had her fizzing with tingles like a sip of champagne.

"Well, you won me over when we first met, rescuing me from the ribbon-of-death and all." She offered him a coy smile. "But, after what happened yesterday, I wondered what your real intentions were. I thought you might be a game-player, wanting to compete in more than just the swimming pool." Zen shook her head, a look of puzzlement on her face as she shrugged. "Now, after talking to you, discovering more about you, I'm back to square one again."

"Does that mean you're back to liking me?" The mischievous lilt in his voice had her smile widening. "Maybe even liking me more than when you used to have a poster of me up on your bedroom wall?"

"I wouldn't go that far, but I can see there's a lot to like about you. I also think we've got more in common than I first realized."

"Please elaborate," he told her. "I'm always interested in hearing compliments about myself."

Zen chuckled and nodded in his direction. "Like that, for example. Got to love someone with a good sense of humor."

He cocked a dark eyebrow at her choice of words and had her laughing again.

"You know what I mean," she amended. "You're a very happy person. You seem positive and understanding, as though you're ready to tackle whatever life throws at you. It's a trait I pride myself in as well. I'm always about the positive mental attitude."

"That's the athlete's mindset right there." He aimed an index finger her way. "I can see all those early mornings of high school swimming training have left their mark."

"And all of the softball training, and all of the netball training, and all the others." Smiling, she leaned her elbows on the tabletop. "It's one of the main reasons my grandfather left me Poseidon's Shore. He saw how much I loved sports and how passionate I became about bettering myself and striving to reach a goal. It wasn't about winning for me, only about working hard to beat my own personal best and show myself what I was made of. That's what made me want to create a place where I could encourage others to test their boundaries and achieve their dreams as well." Feeling her cheeks heat from all the indulgent self-talk, Zen fidgeted distractedly with her long ponytail.

"That's pretty inspiring," Seb praised.

"No." She shook her head. "It's nothing compared to what you've achieved, Seb. Even if you decide to retire, you're still making a difference. You're inspiring people every day just by being yourself."

"So are you."

Embarrassed, Zen glanced away, but when Seb reached across the table for her hand, she let him take it, allowing him to caress the back reassuringly. The affection pulled at something inside of her and she found herself looking back at him again.

"I'm serious, Zenia. I'm not throwing out empty compliments to win you over, I swear. I really mean it. I see how you talk to people, even with your family, your sister. It's within you, this force of support and motivation." While he spoke, as though remembering, a spark of wonder flickered in his eyes and creased the corner of his smile. "Your sweet, genuine nature makes it easier for people to believe when you tell them they can achieve anything, that their dreams are attainable. I saw it yesterday when you were talking to new clients. You honestly want to help them triumph in whatever goals they set for themselves. It's really admirable and much more selfless than what goes on in my world of glitzy functions and media exploits."

As her cheeks heated under his tender stare and her heart swelled at his kind, compassionate words, Zen noticed her vision blurring, eyes brimming a little with damp tears. She wiped at them and laughed away the emotion tugging painfully at her chest. It was nice to be seen, to have her passion understood, like the way her beloved grandfather had seen and understood her.

"Wasn't I supposed to be the one paying you compliments?" She blinked moist lashes, clearing her cloudy sight.

"I compliment where compliments are due," Seb smiled and it seemed to hold a deeper meaning this time, something heartfelt and real.

Nerves had Zen inhaling sharply, breath catching in her throat as her mouth went dry, her fingers cold. She felt tossed about in a twister of emotions. One-minute Seb was someone she craved, a celebrity she lusted after, the next he was off limits, dating her sister and now, she could easily see him winning her heart. It was crazy, they barely knew each other, even after their lengthy conversation.

Yet, their connection was evident, their chemistry strong, much like the elusive spark people spend their whole single life searching for. Zen hadn't expected it with him, to feel this way, especially not after yesterday's press conference of falsities, but it had happened anyway.

She stared at him and he at her, their smiles widening as seconds ticked by, as though they were privy to some mystical secret. Zen's thoughts raced, questioning new feelings that were bursting to life, making her heart lift like a helium-filled balloon, while her sensible nature tried to drag her down with reality at every peak. Anxiousness had her laughing again and Seb joined her, breaking the sizzling attraction that had been building between them.

"We should probably head back," Zen began reluctantly, inching her hand free of his. But, before she could say any more, she found herself diverted by a familiar female voice.

"Sebastian? You-hoo! I thought that was you." With a gregarious wave, Lexy skipped keenly over to their table and slipped into the empty chair beside Seb. "We've been looking for you all morning. You must have your phone on silent, silly."

"We?" Seb questioned warily.

Preoccupied with Lexy's vivacious entrance, neither Zen nor Seb noticed Emmett's arrival until he plonked down into another empty chair next to them.

"For God's sake, Sebastian," his agent chided. "When you leave me a note saying you've gone to do a few laps, I don't expect you to disappear on me for over four hours."

"I haven't disappeared, Emmett," Seb refuted. "I'm right here and I'm not needed for anything until eleven-thirty."

"Not needed for anything?" Flabbergasted, Emmett spat the words. He aimed his palms out like stop signs. "My phone has been burning up with calls and texts since last night. Everyone who's anyone in the media industry wants the gossip on what's quickly becoming known as

Slexy."

"On what?" Clearly unimpressed, Seb slumped back, smoothing his black t-shirt before linking his fingers over his taut stomach.

"It's a celebrity thing," Lexy piped in. "A blending of names to signify the union of a trendy couple."

Confused, Seb shrugged. "And?"

"It's us," she exclaimed. "Seb and Lexy. *Slexy.* Don't you love it?"

Seb's repulsed sneer of lips said it all.

When Lexy tried to explain further, Emmett sliced his hand through the air to silence her.

"It doesn't matter, Sebastian. What matters is the increased media hype, a new wave of fans. This will surely bolster your stagnating career, buddy. It's what we were hoping for." Emmett's grin split his face in two.

"It's what *you* were hoping for, Emmett." Seb raised his chin. "And my career is not stagnating just because I'm considering retiring from competing."

"Shh," Emmett shushed him, signaling for Seb to be silent while he quickly assessed the crowd of people around them. "You can't say things like that out in the open, Sebastian. Anyone could hear you."

"I didn't realize it was a secret, Emmett."

Seb's agent glared at him.

Feeling uneasy and suddenly like the fourth-wheel, Zen pushed her chair back from the table and stood. "I think it's time I go tend to things back at the gym."

"Yes, yes." Emmett dismissed her with another hand gesture and turned back to his client. "We need to work out a game plan, Sebastian. We should de—"

"You don't have to leave, Zenia." Seb cut his agent off. "I think we have a lot more to talk about, don't you?"

"Like what?" Lexy queried nosily as she tossed a look between them.

"Yes, Seb," Emmett agreed. "Like what?"

Zen swallowed apprehensively under the intense stares,

feeling like a wounded pigeon in the hyena cage. She shook her whole body in response as though every inch of her was dismissing the notion. "It doesn't matter. Maybe another time," she told them all.

"Zen?" Seb's pleading tone yanked at her insides, compelling her, but she ignored it.

"Maybe later," she said again, but knew it felt like a lie.

She offered him a docile wave, the other two a weakened smile and then slipped away, hearing Emmett's enthusiastic conversation begin again on her departure.

It was undeniable her and Seb shared a special bond, with the possibility of something more growing between them, but something was still off, it felt unbalanced. Maybe it wasn't their time. He was still deciding the next path in his career, while she had begun hers, and what he had with Lexy—what Emmett was encouraging his client to build—was not something Zen wanted to compete with. She didn't know how Lexy truly felt, but Zen wasn't the type of person to interfere with a relationship, especially one involving her sister.

No. Maybe she'd fallen into that trap once again— allowed herself to acknowledge her blossoming feelings for Seb without properly thinking the situation through. He could do as he wanted, what Emmett instructed, he didn't owe her anything. But it was going to be hard for Zen to see him getting cozy with her sister, when she longed to be in that position herself.

CHAPTER 7

The warm golden lights of the living room illuminated the large, tropically decorated space, as the wide-screen television on the far wall flashed hypnotically with fluctuating images. The buzz, click and garbled speech of rapidly changing channels competed with the calming swoosh of small cyclic waves, crashing on the shoreline outside. Salty sea air and the fragrance of nearby frangipanis wafted in, giving the room a lingering scent of summer holidays, even though the season had recently passed.

Lounging on the sapphire-blue sofa, Seb nursed a half-devoured bowl of popcorn on his lap, picking from it intermittently and tossing pieces in his mouth. He fiddled with the remote, pressing buttons, and flicking through the evening's programs, altering the sound. He felt unsettled, regretful of how the day had transpired and had said prayer after silent prayer wishing he'd left the café when Zen had. If he had, perhaps she would have spent the rest of the day with him. Maybe they could have eaten lunch together. Even dinner.

As it was, he'd barely seen her for the rest of the day. There had been a flash of her at the beginning of the workshop when she'd introduced him and he'd seen her briefly when it had come to a close, but that had been it. The rest of the time, she seemed to be avoiding him. The idea of it niggled at him, eating at him like ants chewing through his skin. He'd felt a real connection with her this morning just as he had the day they'd met. He craved to spend more time with her and get to know more about her, but everyone and everything seemed to be working against him.

Emmett wanted him to spend more time with Lexy, while she in turn longed to be latched parasitically to Seb's side, and everyone else seemed desperate for his focused attention. Usually, he wasn't bothered by it. He often gave his fans what they wanted, spending time with them to show his appreciation of their support, and frequently enjoyed it. But, now? It was like his mind was infected. It was a constant effort not to think about Zenia and to stop himself from seeking her out. He'd never experienced such an absorbing distraction before and yet, he didn't want it to end. His desire to be around her was like a craving, an addiction he couldn't give up. He felt content and happier when in her presence, as though she held some magic switch that calmed him, releasing all his worries and giving him hope—a hope for something meaningful beyond the superstar image and gold medals.

"Geez, Sebastian," Emmett groaned as he entered the room. "Are you having some kind of epileptic fit or something? What's with the constant channel surfing? Just pick something and stick with it."

Seb growled out a sigh and plopped the remote on the coffee table beside him, leaving the television on a news station.

"In other celebrity news," the female anchor on screen announced to her audience watching from home.

Seb reached for the remote again, but Emmett held up a hand.

"No. Leave it there. I want to see this."

"It looks like our golden boy of swimming, Sebastian DuMont, has attracted more than a few memories during his return to his childhood hometown. After announcing the news of a budding new love affair at yesterday's press conference"—the screen converted to a silent video recording of the media frenzy at Poseidon's Shore Health Club—"Sebastian was seen cozying up to the same blonde woman this afternoon." Again, the image switched and paparazzi-snapped still photographs of Seb and Lexy taken through the gym's picture windows and outdoor fence were shown one after the other on screen.

"I hear you ask, who is this woman?" The newscaster asked her viewers. "Why does she look so familiar? Well, she's no other than Alexis Andino, promising social media influencer and part owner of the Poseidon's Shore Health Club, the same fitness center Sebastian returned home to support. A coincidence? This reporter thinks not and wonders if this lovely lady might be the reason Seb returned home, after all."

As photos from Lexy's social media accounts plastered across the screen, Seb lunged for the remote and turned the television off.

"Hey, spoilsport. It was just getting interesting." Emmett collapsed into the sofa seated across from Seb's and frowned at his client. "Okay, what's up? You've been deflated all afternoon. Tell me what's going on?"

"It's unlikely you'll fix it even if I tell you, so why should I bother?" Seb hugged his arms around the bowl of popcorn and hated that, even with the food filling it, his stomach felt queasy and knotted.

"You should tell me, because I care, Sebastian, and because it's part of my job to keep you happy."

Seb glowered over at him. "Well, you suck at your job."

Emmett's eyes widened, but he visibly pursed his lips, thinking over his words before he answered. "It's not really constructive feedback, but I'll let it slide this time. Come on, buddy, tell me what's with all the pouting?

You're acting like a whiny teenager."

"Well, if you really want to know, Emmett, I feel like shit," he grumbled and then righted his position in the sofa. "And for your information, wanting to be quiet and alone for a couple of hours does not constitute whiny teenage behavior."

"No, but that petulant tone does."

Seb's glare became hostile. "Shut it, Emmett. You're on thin ice as it is right now."

"Me?"

"Yes, you."

"Upset my favorite client?" His eyes grew large with innocence. "It can't be true."

"You know what you've done, Emmett and you keep pushing it. You've essentially trapped me and I don't know what to do."

"Me?" His agent asked again, shaking his head, expression guiltless. "I only ever do things to help you, Sebastian. I'm on your team."

"You're on your own team, Emmett and I've always known it. Normally, we're working toward the same goals, but this time around you've screwed me."

"No. I've done nothing of the sort."

"Cut the crap. This whole relationship thing with Lexy. It's not right."

"Buddy," Emmett soothed. "It doesn't have to be real. It doesn't even have to go for long. It's about igniting your image. Getting the nation talking about you again."

"And why's that? So, I'll feel pressured into signing a new contract. The more the whole nation is talking about me, the easier it is for me to crash and burn, isn't it?"

"Sebastian," his agent tsked at him and shook his head. "I'd never let that happen. Even if you didn't sign with the agency again. We're friends, too. There's no ill will. I want you to do the right thing by yourself. That's what I'm trying to show you—what you could have again with a little tweaking in your life."

"I don't want my life tweaked, Emmett." Seb balled his hands into fists.

"I don't think you really know what you want, Sebastian." Emmett relaxed back into the cushioned sofa and crossed one knee over the other as Seb scowled at him.

"I don't want Lexy and it's not right to abuse her feelings or Zen's in this charade."

"Lexy's in it for the fame, she doesn't care about the romance." Emmett threw up a hand. "And, how are Zenia's feelings being abused? She's not even involved in this."

Seb slid the bowl of popcorn onto the coffee table in front of him and released a blustery sigh as he flopped back and hugged his arms across his chest.

"Hang on," Emmett shot forward, dropping his dangling foot to the floor. "This is what *this* is all about isn't it?" He swirled his hand in Seb's direction. "You like her. You like Zenia and you're mad at me for forcing you to act as though you're close to Lexy? That's it, isn't it?" He slapped the wooden top of the coffee table.

Seb glared at him.

"It seems so obvious now." He chortled and then held his hands up as though halting everything. "But, Seb, you don't even know the girl. You only met her yesterday, spent a few hours talking to her and who knows what sort of truth she's telling. You have to see you're being ridiculous over this. Surely, the benefits of the fantasy relationship with Lexy far outweigh the unlikely possibility with this strange woman you've just met. It's not practical."

"By your reasoning, we should judge Lexy the same," Seb justified. "We did only meet her yesterday as well."

Emmett scoffed. "It's different. Lexy's from our world. It's obvious what she wants and what she'll do to get there. We know the dangers she might pose, and can anticipate them. But, with Zenia, we don't know what she's after. She could really mess you up if you let her, Sebastian, really break you. Do you want that?"

"Zen's not like that."

"How do you know, buddy? You've only just met her."

Shocked at the accusation, Seb grimaced and shook his head. He was certain his agent was wrong, felt to his bones Zenia wasn't like that, but his agent's questioning forced a niggling doubt deep inside. He *had* only met her. It *had* only been two days. Was it really enough to promise the possibility of a deep and meaningful relationship? Was it enough for him to question Emmett—the agent who had worked hard for him for fifteen years, who had become a friend? Or enough to doubt Emmett's new idea of "dating" Lexy to gain more publicity? His agent had suggested similar pretenses in the past and had worked with other agents and celebrities in a similar way to raise public profiles in a mutually beneficial manner.

Seb rubbed his face, scraping his hands down his cheeks. He didn't know what to think, what to do. He liked Zen, he really did, but wariness was part of everyday celebrity survival.

"All I'm saying, Sebastian," Emmett reached for him, patting his shoulder reassuringly, "is you should take a little more time to get to know this woman before making any big changes. We don't want you losing your head, your heart or your millions to her because of a little infatuation, do we?" He caught Seb's worried gaze and held it. "And, if she is the genuine article, then she'll understand what you're doing with Lexy, that it's only work, a part of promoting the product and that product is you. Without the public interest, your adoring fans, and your endorsement deals, you struggle to remain relevant and until your contract has fully expired, it's my job to keep you in the spotlight. You understand?"

For the first time throughout the whole conversation, a sincerity shone through Emmett's gaze. There was honest concern there, even a hint of sympathy and the look tugged at something in Seb's chest, wrenching at the connection, the compassion for an old friend who had never before let him down. It had him sighing again and then he nodded in agreement.

"Yeah, I understand," Seb told him.

CHAPTER 8

Saliva-inducing scents of Mediterranean cuisine swirled with the fresh breeze wafting in through the gaping glass doors of the second story balcony. Treated as the heart of the house, the generously sized, contemporary kitchen and adjacent dining area were where the Andino family always chose to congregate, especially on Mondays, also known as family dinner night. Even though Zen and her sister had moved out several years earlier and now shared their own simple house a street back from the water, their childhood home still held an intimacy and solace unlike any other.

While Zenia, stared out over the darkened water, listening to the cool night air swish through the cotton trees and the soothing waves as they washed in, she pondered over her rather uneventful Monday. As she had yesterday afternoon, Zen had tried to leave Sebastian—and Lexy—in peace. It had been painful to do so, with her nerves twitching, instructing her to look for Seb, and to get closer to him. It was an odd yearning, like the desire to check her phone when waiting on an important call. She knew if she allowed herself, it might become addictive, this constant need to seek Seb out, and be around him. It took all of her strength to push the desire aside and focus back on her work. Although it made matters even more difficult when the guest speaker was the one person she'd been trying to avoid.

A few times today she'd caught herself drifting off into fantasy, losing herself in a daydream where Seb had told the reporters he was interested in *her*, not Lexy. She'd let herself imagine how different her and Seb's relationship might be, before dragging herself back—with the heavy thud of a falling piano—into her current reality. The media and its audience believed it was Lexy that Seb was dating, and Zen knew it wouldn't look good for him or her if that suddenly changed. So, for now, her best option was to keep her distance and contain any feelings that sought to grow just by looking at the handsome hunk of a man.

Zen glanced over her shoulder at the pat of footsteps approaching and saw Lexy offer her a genuinely cheerful smile.

"It's getting chilly out here," Lexy rubbed her bare arms.

Zen nodded. "It's finally starting to feel like autumn."

"So…" Lexy leaned on the railing beside her and stared down at the street below, at the mix of streetlight and shadows.

"So?" Zen questioned with a nod.

Lexy turned to her, expression still lit with merriment. "I've got some exciting news."

Zen smiled and bumped her shoulder affectionately against her sister's. "Do tell, Lex."

Excitement sparkled in Lexy's eyes. "I've invited Seb to family dinner."

Straightening abruptly, Zen shook her head. "Not tonight?"

"Yeah, why? I thought it was a great idea."

"Why didn't you tell me earlier?"

"Because I didn't think it mattered." Lexy's brows drew. "And because I don't need your permission."

"Well, did you get Mum and Dad's?" Zen gestured

inside to where her parents were chatting over food preparation in the kitchen.

"They were fine with it. I thought you'd be, too."

"Well, you thought wrong, Lexy."

"What's your drama, Zen? I thought you'd be happy to have Seb come round. You seem to like him just fine, so what's the problem?"

Zen cast a look down at the quiet street and sighed. "I do like him." *Maybe a little too much*, she pondered and then turned back to her sister. "But we don't know him, not properly. Are you really comfortable having him visit here? Seeing all the old photographs on the wall? Hearing potentially embarrassing stories from Mum and Dad?"

Lexy rejected Zen's questioning with a wave of her hand. "Oh, don't worry. I've already laid down the law with the parentals. No talking about my childhood or any potentially mortifying stories thereof. And any photos of me on display have been hidden in the spare room. I thought you might have noticed."

Zen gulped in a breath. "And what about me? My photos, my stories?"

"Who cares?" Lexy shrugged nonchalantly. "None of that is likely to end up in the media if this sensational relationship goes awry."

With a squeak of distress, trepidation giving her the hot and cold chills, Zen grabbed her sister by the shoulders. "Lexy, what have you done?"

Lexy made a pfft noise with her lips and removed herself from Zen's grasp. "I think you need a glass of wine, Zenia. You're totally overreacting about all this and you look super frazzled. We'll have a nice night, you'll see."

The flash of headlights on the seaside road drew Lexy's concentration for a brief moment and she watched as a car parked outside the house. When she looked back at Zen, her huge grin had returned.

"I think he's here," she announced, saying it loudly enough to garner her mum and dad's attention inside.

"Sebastian's here."

As her sister skipped away, shooting instructions at her mother and father, Zen swallowed back the nervous bile climbing high in her throat. No way in hell was tonight going to be *nice*. With Lexy safely removing her past self from the list of conversational topics, Zenia now found herself on the proverbial chopping block as it were and knew she was certain to experience some heavy humiliation. Lexy had been right about one thing though. Zen definitely needed a glass of wine—or four.

CHAPTER 9

Although the mouthwatering smells of dinner still lingered in the air, the dining room table—previously cluttered with moussaka, green salad and buttered bread—had been emptied, cleaned and left with the after-dinner drinks of tea, coffee and water. Dessert was a tray of Tim-Tams, which Zen's mother had apologized profusely for, giving her younger daughter a chiding look whenever anyone took one of the chocolate-covered, store-bought biscuits.

With the night drawing on, the luminous lights of the kitchen dimmed, the gathering began to feel somewhat more intimate. After all the talk shared, the impassioned discussions, the jovial humor and the expected reminiscences, there seemed an easiness now. Where the atmosphere initially prickled with mystery and tenseness, it had dispelled and left a comforting feeling of familiarity. It felt cozy, warming both the heart and soul, and had made Zen consider forgiving her sister's hasty dinner invitation to the celebrity crush of her dreams.

When her husband snatched his third Tim-Tam of the evening, Zen's mother once again huffed her displeasure.

"If only I had known earlier that we were to have

company tonight, I would have baked something special. But, my daughter, she only tells me when she arrives for dinner. It was a surprise, she said. But surprise—we have no dessert."

Zenia stifled a chuckle as her sister grumbled.

"Oh, leave it, Mum. No one cares that you didn't bake. You know Zen and I rarely eat dessert anyway."

"Sebastian might care?" Gabriella pointed her nose skyward.

"I'd never turn down something sweet, Mrs. Andino," Seb added charmingly. "Perhaps I could attend another family dinner in the future? That way I'll have the opportunity to try your special dessert."

Gabriella's face radiated with pleasure. "Next Monday. It is a deal, and please, we are Gabriella and Leo." She pointed to herself then her husband.

"That's only if you're still in town." Zen piped up, watching Seb closely. She didn't want him promising something he couldn't deliver on. "I thought you were only here for a week."

"I have the power to extend our stay if I want to." He winked at her and there was something hidden in his expression, as though the subject was one he'd considered before.

"Well, I hope you stay indefinitely." Lexy cuddled up to him from her seat beside his at the head of the table. "Either that or you take me back to Sydney with you."

"Lexy would love to visit Sydney," Gabriella gushed.

Leo shook his head at his wife. "Don't pressure the boy, Gabriella. He's only just met her. You don't need to suggest they run off interstate together."

"Seb, doesn't mind, Daddy." Lexy fluttered her lashes at the swim star. "In fact, his agent, Emmett, has already suggested that might be a possibility."

"*He has?*" It was said in chorus by everyone else in the room, though tone and interest levels varied.

Zen felt her stomach flip-flop at the discovery and

balled her hands into tight fists beneath the table in an effort to calm down. If Seb and Lexy were to fly off to Sydney together then so be it. There was nothing she could do, and—besides her mounting infatuation with the real-life Sebastian DuMont, not only the poster boy from her youth—there was nothing she should do. No matter how she truly felt about him inside, they were yet to become anything more than business associates on the cusp of friendship. She had about as much right to tell him what he should do with his romantic life as she did to tell him which underwear to buy. Her best bet was to stay away from him where she could, leave things platonic, and keep her heart and emotional wellbeing safe.

"This is news to me," Seb told her, slipping free of Lexy's embrace. "All I've discussed with him is the possibility of staying in Sandgate a while longer."

Lexy rebuffed Seb's concern with a pat to his muscular chest. "Don't stress over it, Sebastian. He only mentioned it to me this afternoon and told me he'd speak to you later about it. He obviously hasn't had the chance." She gave him a charismatic grin much like his own.

"Obviously." Seb's instinctive smile suggested one thing, while his suspicious lilt said another.

His gaze connected with Zen's for an instant and he tried to hold it, to communicate something, but she forced herself to look away. It was like looking at an eclipse, the vision of his attractive face, those sexy, chiseled features captivating her, capturing her until she could will herself to break free.

"Well, I'm sorry to say it," Seb addressed the group as he pushed himself to his feet, "but, I think it's time for me to call it a night. Zen and I have an early start tomorrow morning. A bootcamp class, if I remember correctly. So, I'll need all the sleep I can get."

"Of course," Leo nodded, following Seb's lead and standing. "And thank you for joining us this evening. It was very entertaining."

Something sparkled in Zen's father's eyes and she wondered if there was more than the usual meaning behind his words.

"We'll look forward to your visit next Monday then, Sebastian" Gabriella told him, rising and hurrying over to him. "Before you leave, what is your favorite dessert?"

"I'll love whatever you choose to make me." Seb touched her affectionately on the shoulder.

"That won't do, young man," Leo chortled. "With Gabriella and cooking, it's best to be specific."

"Okay," Seb tilted his head in thought, laughing nervously. "Um…I'm partial to apple-pie, but honestly whatever's going is fine."

"All right," Gabriella bowed her head in agreement. "I make apple and almond."

"Okay," Seb said again, becoming flustered. "Thank you." It sounded more like a question.

"Bye, then." Lexy lunged for him, planting a kiss on his cheek before Seb had time to notice her attack.

He jerked away from her, startled, with a look of horror in his wide eyes. Blinking rapidly, he gave another anxious laugh and moved away from her, casting a glance at her parents instead.

"Thanks again," he blurted and began backing toward the stairs to the lower level. After a couple of stumbled steps, he stopped. "Actually"—he turned his attention to Zenia—"would you mind walking me out, Zen? I have a few questions to ask you about tomorrow."

Standing behind the dining table as though for protection, Zen gawped at him and coughed out her surprise.

"She'd love to," Leo accepted, moving back to grab his daughter's arm, dragging her forward.

"Um…" Zen knew it was a bad idea, but couldn't find the right words to say to turn Sebastian down.

"Hurry up, Zen," Lexy groaned, becoming irritated. "Seb needs to get home to get his beauty sleep. It's the least you can do, since it's your fault he has to get up so early tomorrow."

"Ah…" Zen gasped as her father released her arm brusquely, plonking her like a delivery in front of Sebastian.

"Shall we?" Seb asked, extending his own arm to her.

Zen glanced back at her family, but only her father was watching them now, a curiousness in his eyes. Her mother and Lexy had moved back to the table and were having their own hushed conversation.

"Fine," Zen growled out her displeasure and ignored Seb's outstretched arm, descending the stairs on her own ahead of him instead.

On the lower floor, after striding hurriedly to the front door and opening it in preparation of ending the awkward encounter as quick as possible, she looked up at him.

"Okay, what are your questions?" She asked him.

He stopped in front of her, shadowing her with his height, staring deeply into her eyes, his gaze drifting to her mouth and back up again. As she lost herself in the dark brown of his perfect irises, the scent of him, and the heat radiating from his chest, Zen felt her body respond to his, opening the floodgates of increasing fascination and dangerous emotions. Tingling sensations flared through her nerve endings, sparking to life all the delectably sensuous feelings of desire. Her breath quickened and with every gulp of air, her chest swelled, pressing against the blue cotton of her blouse, inching closer to him, aching to be touched.

Seb's pupils were endless midnight enthralling her, his lips plumped, desperate to be kissed. Zen knew she'd been lost for mere milliseconds, caught up in desirous chemistry for the briefest of instants, but the response he awakened within her had her wishing it was an eternity. As her heartbeat quivered like the frantic wings of a moth thrilled to finally reach the light, Seb broke the erotic hypnotism of their natural connection and reached for her, clutching her to him as his mouth met hers.

Zen drowned, spellbound in the simple kiss of lips on lips and the sensations it evoked within her. Seb's mouth and body molded to hers as though he had always belonged there. She was overwhelmed, lightheaded and craved so much more of him that when he broke the kiss, releasing her body, she stumbled backward catching herself against the wall behind her.

"Whoa," Sebastian released a breath, the sound both excitement and awe. "I can't believe I waited three days to do that."

"Three days?" Zen blinked at him, touched a hand to her lips as she fought to put her thoughts back in some sort of order.

Seb's tender smile pulled at something in her stomach.

"And I'm not waiting another three before we do it again," he told her, a cheekiness pulling at the corner of his mouth. "Goodnight, Zenia."

Then, he was out the door and down the few front steps in joyful bounds before she was able to mutter her own goodbye.

CHAPTER 10

Within the grounds of the Poseidon's Shore Health Club was an expanse of green parkland, which spread out alongside the outdoor swimming pool and stretched up to a grassy hillside overlooking the bay water. Gnarled cotton trees lined the edges of the otherwise vacant lawn, providing a shady site to leash furry friends while working out outside. Zen's pooch, Melrose, and a few wet-nosed companions brought along by those attending the early Tuesday bootcamp session, sniffed each other and lounged on the dew-laden grass. Occasionally, they offered an encouraging bark and excited waggling tail when seeing their owners' enthusiastic participation in the exercise activities.

The ascending sunlight grew in luster and heat, thawing sleepy bodies and heavy muscles, and glinting off the nearby pool water as it splashed and stirred with the motivated lap swimmers.

Having already been at the bootcamp class for nearly an hour, the group—with Sebastian at the helm—had moved on tirelessly from their warm up and through their first interval training routine. Although the workout schedule had been planned days earlier, Seb delighted in the fact that the next assignment of paired kickboxing required those in the class to pick a partner, and he knew exactly whom he'd choose.

While they had essentially been running the session together—with Seb instructing and Zenia assisting—Zen had barely said a word to him that wasn't in some way related to the class at hand or in relation to the center's opening week program. Seb had hoped last night's kiss might have had her buzzing with sensual chemistry and anticipation, eager to do it all over again, just as he was, but she'd yet to give him that indication. He supposed he was to blame for her desiring to keep her distance.

After being shackled in a contrived relationship with Lexy and the drama that induced, he'd given Zen the mother of all mixed signals. Yet, even when she was acting distant, her nearness set him on fire. It was something he'd clicked onto last night, that this connection they shared seemed so ingrained in both of them, and wouldn't go away on its own. He'd decided then and there to take the risk and follow his instincts, even after everything Emmett had said to him. In Seb's mind, his incredible kiss with Zen and all it had kindled within him, had reconfirmed that he'd made the right decision.

As Zenia passed him, heading to the pile of torso-sized strike pads and boxing gloves they had organized earlier, Sebastian reached out and grabbed her hand, pulling her beside him, both of them facing the class. While her expression contorted with shock and reprimand, she didn't fight him.

"It's time to pick your gear and your partner," Seb addressed the group, tossing a smile down his shoulder at Zen. "Then line up, opposite each other, one person with the pad, one with the gloves, and Zen and I will demonstrate the first set."

As the joyful crew of exercise-enthusiasts followed instructions, Seb finally released Zen's hand and narrowed his gaze playfully. "So, partner, which one of us gets the gloves first? I'll let you decide."

With a glare, Zen pursed her lips, but didn't say anything as she moved to retrieve a set of kickboxing equipment of her own. Upon her return, she tossed him the chunky, plastic-covered pad. The force of her throw hit his black singlet-clad stomach with a thud before he caught it.

"I take it I'm in for a beating," Seb chuckled.

"You told me I could decide who gets hit first," Zen told him. "I choose you."

"Bring it on." His smile widened as he lifted the strike pad, holding it like a shield in front of him.

When Zen had her scarlet-red gloves on and had tightened the Velcro straps around her wrists, Seb looked back at the group, now in two lines, facing each other, looking fierce and pumped, ready and waiting for the set to begin.

"We'll start with single punches," he explained. "Five with the right, five with the left and hold. Zen, will you give us a demonstration, please?"

"Of course." For the first time all morning, she grinned at him.

Throughout the early hours of daylight, she'd smiled at members of their class, at her golden retriever, Mel and even the other dogs, but purposely not at him. Seb was both elated at the happier, kinder expression and partially nervous, for as her lips spread, expression beaming with pleasure and mischief, Zen sunk into a fighting stance and threw her first right-handed punch. The force of it and the surprising weight behind it had him wobbling, so Seb bent his knees even lower, digging his feet into the ground in preparation for the second.

Zen pounded her fist into the big, spongy pad again and again, each whack pushing Seb's shoulders and upper body back with the momentum, his biceps bulging as he fought to keep the protective gear in place. Finishing five, she switched her feet, altering her posture and started on the next set with her left. Each time a grunt of exertion or a huffed exhale left Seb's lips, Zen's grin grew larger. Once she'd completed the display with her final punch, she straightened and gave Seb a look of satisfaction when he sighed in relief and did the same.

"There you have it," he told the attentive gathering, puffing slightly. "Now, it's your turn, but remember it's technique over speed."

As those in the bootcamp class began pummeling their partners, the thuds and slaps on the pads mixing with laughter and chatter, Seb turned to Zenia.

"If I'm not mistaken, you were trying to topple me." He eyed her warily.

Grin still wide, she shrugged. "It was worth a try."

"And if I had actually fallen over?" He asked.

Impishness twinkled in her dark gaze. "I would have laughed and thought the karma had been well deserved."

"It's not exactly karma when you're the one hitting me," Seb teased, nodding at her boxing gloves.

"No," she bunted her gloved fists together. "But maybe it would have made you think twice the next time you went to kiss me without my permission."

"So, you're sore about that then? I thought it might still have to do with the Lexy thing."

Zen tilted her head. "All of the above."

When he went to answer her, she pointed a glove-covered hand at their audience and Seb quickly realized the walloping sounds of punching had stopped.

"Well done, everyone," he praised. "Now, we move on to doubles. We'll do ten of them. Zen, if you would?" He nodded at her and sunk into a stronger stance as she did the same.

Her amused grin returned as she steadied herself and began the first five, beating a quick repetition of right, left, right, left into the strike pad. With that lot complete, having still not tumbled Sebastian, she changed position and altered the hit to a swift left, right, left, right.

After Zen's final punch, Seb drew in a deep breath and gestured to the two lines of people before him. "Okay? Ready?"

The thrashing beat of boxing began again and Seb looked over at Zen, who was watching him as though waiting for him to continue their quiet discussion.

"So, all of the above?" He questioned her and got a nod in response. Frowning, he stepped closer to her. "Look, Zen, I'm sorry if I've been a little hot and cold. I've been conflicted over the last few days, especially considering everything." He glanced into the distance, contemplating Emmett's words about the benefits of acting close with Lexy, about being more careful with Zen and then shook the thoughts away. When his gaze met Zenia's again, he pushed the tenderness he felt for her into his expression. "But I'd like to see where this goes, this special bond between *us*. I like you, Zenia—I enjoy being around you—and I'm pretty certain you like me, too."

"And the *Lexy thing*?" She queried, throwing his term back at him in a clever sassy tone.

The pounding thuds of the rhythmic punching petered out and then halted altogether drawing Seb's attention. Pausing again in his awkward conversation with Zen, he faced the bootcampers.

"Next, we move on to uppercuts," he explained and held the strike pad out and facing down. "Let's do five on each side and ten quicks together." As he lowered in position, Seb glanced at Zen and nodded for her to begin.

Knees bent, with her left leg back, feet with a fixed grip on the ground, Zen angled her fist and punched upward into the cushioned pad held at chin-height before her. She did the set unhurriedly, demonstrating correct technique, before altering her stance and completing five with her left fist. Then she returned to her dominant pose, feet slightly closer together and rapidly fired ten punches, right, left, right, left as Seb fought to keep the bag steady and facedown. He released a long breath when she'd finished, realizing he'd been holding it with all the exertion and noticed that his arms tingled with numbness from the constant physical abuse.

"It's your turn now, team," he told the fit men and women in the bootcamp crew. "Show us what you've got."

When the thwack of boxing gloves against the pads erupted again, melding with pants of exhaustion and chuckles of good-humor, Seb and Zen drew closer to each other.

"Well, Sebastian," Zen quirked a dark eyebrow at him. "Have you got an answer for me?"

He freed a hand from the strap at the back of the strike pad and laid it reassuringly on Zen's shoulder. "I wish it had never happened," he told her, "that it wasn't happening now. I know I need to get myself out of this mess with Lexy, but I haven't yet figured out how. All I know is that I don't want to lose you or what we might have in the meantime, while this charade is going on." He slid his hand to her neck, caressing the soft skin there, stroking his thumb over her collarbone, relishing in the contact, the intimacy of the connection. "Like I said, Zen"—he stared into her dark brown eyes—"I like you. I really do. Who cares if we don't yet know each other? If we give ourselves a chance, spend some actual time together, we'll answer those questions, break down those walls. I'm ready and willing to give it a try, if you are."

The thunderous whacking of the final set of punches prompted Seb to check in on their class. Seeing many people had completed the task or were about to, he waited the final few seconds and chose to address them again.

"Great job, everyone," he commended, taking his hand from atop Zen's shoulder to slap it on the foam pad as though in applause. "Before we move on to some leg action, it's time to swap roles." He gestured for the pairs to exchange equipment. "Turn to your partner and find out if they're up for the challenge." Although Seb's tone was humorous, encouraging laughter from the crowd, he hoped it was clear to Zen that his statement held a hidden, more sincere meaning.

He turned to her as the exercise group chatted amongst themselves, readying for the next segment. "What do you think?" He probed quietly, apprehension at the possibility of a *no* making his heartbeat quicken. "Are you?"

She stepped closer to him, the pad the only thing separating them. "Up for the challenge?" Zen's beautiful eyes widened, feigning naivety.

Seb nodded.

With a sigh, she lowered her gaze, glanced around them as though musing over her options. When her eyes met his again, a small smile lingered on her lips, something earnest this time, not hostile, but still with an air of cheekiness. "It's not an ideal situation," she told him.

Seb's heart spluttered like a failing engine.

"But," she continued, "how could I possibly turn down such a proposition, especially when it involves the man whose poster used to hang on my bedroom wall?"

Uncertain if that was her answer or if she was still playing with him, nervousness had Seb holding his breath. Undoing the Velcro straps, Zen tapped her gloved hands roughly to Seb's chest, sitting them atop the kickboxing pad, before pulling her hands free and leaving the boxing gloves balanced there. When he grabbed at the gloves and she grasped hold of the plastic-covered pad, she winked, making his heart skip in anticipation.

"What I'm saying is, I like you, too, Sebastian," she explained, affection shining in her smile. "And, I'm happy to give this a try."

Joy and relief washed over him, causing the tenseness in his chest, to rush away so abruptly and with such force that it made him momentarily lightheaded. Seb stumbled back a step, knees weakening, and losing balance as he wobbled. He might have gone down, his legs threatening to give way, had Zen not—at that exact moment—dropped the kickboxing pad and reached for him, clutching his elbows, giving him time to steady his feet. When he was upright, the bootcamp class still pleasantly oblivious on the lawn next to him, Seb laughed at himself.

"Karma?" He asked Zen.

"Karma." She nodded with jokey certainty and then chuckled along with him.

CHAPTER 11

The silty mudflats of the Sandgate foreshore spanned the length of the footpath-edged parkland and reached out into the distance, to the weak waves of the incoming tide. Canine owners wandered around with dogs of all sorts—lanky, runty, shaggy, slinky. All with dirty feet and sandy bellies as they roamed the muddy brown landscape, bolting, rolling, and scuffling in the joy of being off-leash. Melrose, Zenia's golden retriever, dashed amongst them, tongue lolling and kicking up sand as he bounded to greet his new furry buddies before returning back to his owner and her companion.

It was Thursday afternoon, and Zen and Seb had spent the last few days stealing every spare moment to share some private time with each other. They had talked, opened up and snuck in several steamier kisses, but most of all, they'd grown closer, with the bond they shared securing tighter the more they were together. The only thing that remained in their way, and weighed heavier and heavier on Zen's heart each day, was Seb's public profile "relationship" with her sister and the secrecy that demanded of her own flourishing connection with him.

It might have only been a few days, but she was tired of

feeling like the other woman. Guilt swamped her when Seb was approached by fans who frequently enquired about Lexy, wondering where she was and why he was with Zenia instead. While Lexy hadn't said it in so many words, Zen knew her sister wasn't so concerned about the man or the suggested liaison, but thrived on the celebrity association and the fame that ensued. Even Seb and Emmett had told her as much. Yet, it didn't change the fact that Zen felt as though she were doing something wrong. At the very least, keeping the truth from her parents physically hurt her heart and stressed her out emotionally. She might have kept things hidden from them in the past, but she'd never outright lied, and encouraging them to believe the charade of Lexy dating Seb felt much the same thing.

She drifted closer to Sebastian as they walked barefoot along the damp earth, the lowering sun warming their backs as they headed in toward shore. Mel scampered past them in a blur of gilded fur and swishing tail, chasing after a seagull that had dared to land on his new territory. Seb inched nearer to Zen, closing the gap between them, letting his hand dangle loosely beside hers, almost touching.

He glanced at her, his expression illuminated with cheer and contentedness. "I'd love to hold your hand," he told her.

"It's not difficult," she lifted a shoulder half-heartedly, her pinkie-finger knocking his as their arms swayed. "You slide your palm against mine and let our fingers intertwine."

"So simple," he agreed, "if we weren't in public."

She quickened her stride, crossing in front of him before turning to look at him, taking a few backward steps toward their destination. "You could fix that problem with a simple truth."

He caught up to her as she spun around, coming up on her other side, the back of his hand tickling hers for an instant. "I've told you how much I want to, how I can't wait for this whole debacle to end, but every time I talk to Emmett about it, he convinces me to hold out a bit longer."

Zen quirked an eyebrow at him in protest, knowing full well that Emmett's intentions on this matter had never been entirely pure.

"I know you think he doesn't like you, that all of this with Lexy is another way for him to get me to commit to a new contract I'm not interested in. Believe me, I've already questioned his motives a number of times," Seb released a scoffing laugh. "But he's been my agent for fifteen years and he's never let me down, Zen. He's assured me I can call the relationship quits after a fortnight, that, if I can hold off until then, Lexy and I will both be able to go our separate ways amicably, unscathed by the tabloids and with bolstered profiles. It might not be something I care about at this stage in my career, but it's better that than the alternative, don't you think?"

She couldn't answer him. She knew he trusted Emmett, and had a brotherly relationship with him, but what difference was there between ending the fake relationship after one week or two? Had Emmett actually explained that to him? And, would it really be enough or would Emmett decide longer was better and convince Seb of the same?

Zen believed Seb wasn't the sort of guy who could be easily led into ridiculous schemes and that, if Emmett tried to pressure him into stretching the charade longer, Seb would eventually catch on. But would their budding relationship last through it? Could she keep hiding the truth from her friends and family, keep securing their secret for as long as it might take for Seb to tell Emmett and Lexy it was over? Could she really wait that long, living a lie?

As her silence lengthened and Seb's patient, but intense stare began to burn her cheeks, Zen searched for a suitable answer that wasn't the hurtful truth or another blatant lie. Before she could pull something from the ether, Seb darted in front of her, forcing her to pause her stride.

"Zenia?" His tone had a desperate lilt to it as he placed a hand on her shoulder—a friendly touch, nothing too intimate. "You agree with me, don't you? It's not going to be forever. Another week will be a struggle in itself, but I don't want to let Emmett down." He edged closer, sneaking his hand a little higher, allowing the contact to become slightly sensual as he neared her neck. "Most of all, Zen, I don't want to let you down. I need to know you're okay with this, that we'll get through it together."

She swallowed, her throat suddenly arid and thick. "And if I'm not?" It was a pained whisper.

Seb's eyes flashed wider. He'd taken a step toward her before thinking of the ramifications their closeness might cause, the realization dawning across his face only seconds later, but he didn't move back.

"Zen, please don't say that," he pleaded, tightening his grip securely on her shoulder as though fearful she'd leave. "There's something special between us. I know you feel the same way."

"I'm not saying we don't share a special connection, Seb, or that I don't care for you. I do. With all my heart, I do." As she watched the tense worry ease out of his expression, a small smile replacing it, Zen reached up and pulled Seb's hand from her shoulder, holding it in hers, enjoying the solidness of it, the warmth. "But I'm not made for all these secrets, Sebastian. It's not me. The guilt eats away at me daily. It's souring what we could have, the happiness we could share. I want us to be free to be together, no pretense, no hiding. I long for us to just be *us*."

"So, do I, Zen." There was a tenderness in his eyes as he pulled their linked hands to his chest, covering his heart. "It's all I've wanted since meeting you. A chance for us to be together, to see where it goes, and find out what kind of future we could have." He shook his head as though regretful. "I never expected to be drawn into this mess or to drag you into it with me. It just happened."

"With Emmett's help," Zen muttered.

"You're not wrong," He sighed. "If Emmett hadn't pushed it, I never would have gone along with this charade in the first place. After all, it was you who stole my heart from the very beginning all gift-wrapped and cute in that ceremonial ribbon." His smile widened and a mischievousness twinkled in his eyes.

Zen fought the smirk pulling at her lips, hoping to keep the conversation focused on the more serious topic. "But we are in this mess, Seb, and I don't know if I can keep up the façade." She stole her hand back from his, slid it over his chest, up his neck to cup his chiseled jaw. When he leaned into her touch, she weakened and smiled. "God, I want to kiss you," she pined, lovingly. "I should be able to kiss my boyfriend."

"Boyfriend?" Seb tittered, excited and amused by the word.

"Yes, boyfriend," Zen glared at him playfully. "Do you have a problem with that?"

"No," he beamed and seemed to forget himself for an instant, sneaking his hands over her hips, pulling her closer. "Does that mean you're my girlfriend?"

She nodded authoritatively as she slid her arms around his neck. "That's generally how it goes."

He dipped his head, lips hovering above hers. "Then I absolutely agree. Kissing your boyfriend and being kissed by him is completely mandatory."

Zen's heart leapt, lifting like a kite soaring on an elevating breeze, sensation of invigoration, mixed with lust and affection, making her whole body feel weightless and light. She couldn't believe it. Was he really about to kiss her in public? Were they about to move past all the secrets and lies and finally be free?

Seb inched closer, his warm breath tickling her skin, his

lips almost brushing hers. Zen closed her eyes, giving in to the freedom of the embrace, to the feeling of contentment and glee that tingled through her. As her mouth barely met his, there was a shout, a gruff voice, and Mel barked, disgruntled by the abrupt sound disturbing his play.

"Sebastian!"

There it was again, a deep bellow, forcing Seb and Zen to pull back, out of each other's arms to look around, searching for the owner of the obscured voice.

As they turned, looking to shore, Mel leaning against Zen's bare leg, they noticed a figure standing above the concrete steps waving at them. The person was tall, masculine, and appeared to be well dressed.

"Emmett," Seb groaned.

"How did he know we were out here?" Zen frowned as she patted Mel's soft, furry head.

"I told him I was going for a walk out on the mudflats. I didn't think he'd come looking for me. He doesn't like to get dirty."

"He didn't have to, did he?" Zen derided. "Apparently, screaming your name and alerting everyone in a half mile radius to your presence is okay. Now everyone will be watching us when we get back to shore. I hope you've got your autographing pen ready." She released a weak laugh and took a step forward.

He grabbed her arm, stopping her. "Who says we have to go back that way?"

"Obviously your agent does." Zen gestured to where Emmett was still waving, rather half-heartedly now.

"Well, maybe it's time for Emmett to learn things don't always go his way." With a sassy grin, Seb slipped his arm through hers and pulled her away from their previous destination, moving in a direction parallel to the coastal footpath.

As Mel yipped and followed suit, prancing ahead of them along the damp, silty ground, Zen rested her head against Seb's muscular upper arm, enjoying the feel of him so close and this short extra snippet of time they had together.

CHAPTER 12

Zenia's office within the Poseidon's Shore Health Club was boxy, but well-lit with brightly painted blue and yellow feature walls contrasting against their icy white counterparts. A couple of motivational posters had been framed and secured to the walls, while a desktop computer and neat piles of paper crested the chunky, ivory desk. With the door to the reception desk and main gymnasium closed, the space was relatively quiet and still comfortably air-conditioned. Only a small window gave any indication of what was going on in the world outside the cozy room.

Yet, Zen and Seb were in no mind to care. After their walk along the beach with Mel, having slipped free of Emmett's demands from the shoreside, they'd been lost in their own bubble of amorousness and infatuation. They'd snuck back into the health club via the locked staff entrance at the back of the complex, both high on a chirpy, giggly cloud. The combination of disobeying Emmett and giving into their desire for each other without the hinderance of the public farce, had given them a feeling of liberty and invincibility. While neither of them had actually said it out loud, Zen hoped that this might finally mean an end to the burden of lies that had been weighing heavily on her shoulders.

With the office door shut tightly behind them, Sebastian hugged Zen close and covered her mouth with his. His deep kiss was mesmerizing, tugging at Zen's self-restraint making her want to do more than just kiss him while all alone together in the private room. Her body ached deliciously for him, a feeling at her core yearning for a deeper, more intimate touch as he roamed his hands over her hips and bottom, pulling her snug against him. He groaned into her mouth as the solidness of him met the heated softness of her, dragging a moan from her own lips. They were so caught up in this fireball of lust, all-consuming passion snuffing out any remaining sense, that when a knock pounded at the door, it didn't quite register and didn't stop them. It wasn't until the telling click of the door opening inward that they swiftly broke apart.

"What the hell do you think you're doing?" Emmett barged into the room, slamming the door behind him.

"Excuse me?" Zen exclaimed, breath still short and quick from the intimate encounter. "This is my office, Emmett. I expect privacy unless you knock and are invited in."

"I did knock," he growled at her, slamming his hands on his hips.

"Maybe, but I didn't give you permission to enter."

He glowered at her, looking down his nose, staring at her as though she were an infuriating mosquito droning around his ear.

"What do you want, Emmett?" Seb asked, his tone a little cold as he adjusted his crumpled clothing.

Releasing a crotchety exhale of breath, Emmett dismissed Zen with a sharp hand gesture and focused in on Sebastian, stalking his way over to him.

"What do you think you're doing, Sebastian? You're not listening to me now? You'd rather run down the beach to get away from me? What's wrong with you?" Emmett roared, throwing his hands skyward. He paced away a few quick steps and then back again, stopping to pause and point. "Do you know what you both looked like out there? You looked like a couple, that's what. How is that supposed to help our cause? How are we supposed to smooth that over if the media gets a hold of a photo of the two of you?" He raked his fingers through his hair, fisted them there and then tossed his hands down again. "One week, Sebastian. I asked you for one extra week and you can't even wait that long?"

"Why, Emmett? Why one more week?" Seb argued, moving back to perch on Zen's desk. "Can't we cut our losses and move on?" He gestured to Zen and back to himself. "We're tired of living this lie. We want to be together."

A crazy smile spread Emmett's lips as he nodded. "Do you? Well, that's peachy. But did you ever stop to think how the media will take this when they find out?" He looked into the distance, using his hands to spell out invisible newspaper headlines. *Sebastian DuMont dating Lexy Andino's sister. Superstar Seb moves fast—in and out of the pool. DuMont's two for two with the Andino sisters.* Emmett glared at both of them, resting his hands at his hips again. "I told you, you have to play this smart or they'll crucify you."

"Can't we tell them the truth?" Zen crossed her arms and slipped closer to Seb. "Say that Seb and Lexy never got that close, they're only friends and that it's always been Seb and me from the beginning?"

"Sorry, Zenia, how long have you been working in the media industry?" Emmett raised his index finger, his expression a feigned ponderance. "Do you have twenty years of experience under your belt? How about the fact that I've been looking out for Seb since he was a teenager? You think it might give me some authority on the matter? Do you think I might know what I'm talking about?" His voice raised higher with each query until his rage shone through his eyes and spasmed at his lips.

He groaned with frustration and stomped away, releasing a lengthy puff of breath, reminding Zenia of the squeal of a boiled kettle, only a few octaves lower. His childish tantrum made her want to throw in a few snarky quips of her own, but she knew that would only escalate matters. To talk any sense with him, they had to wait for him to calm.

When Emmett turned around, eyes ablaze, but simmering now, Zen clutched Seb's hand, taking comfort in the tender, fleshy connection.

"Here's what we're going to do," Emmett told them, gaze narrowing as he concentrated in on his thoughts. "I've arranged for you and Lexy to attend the South-East Athletes Charity Gala on Saturday night." He pointed at Seb. "I'd initially turned down the invite as we were supposed be out of town by that point, but as we're staying, we may as well make the most of it." He sighed, obviously irritated and exhausted. "If you can be on your best behavior, be friendly with Lexy, maybe we can get past this without further drama. Let's hope no one took advantage of the situation today and took any incriminating photos as the tabloids and gossip media would eat it up."

"I'd like Zen to come to the Gala, too." Seb interjected, his tone no-nonsense.

"What?" Disbelief had Emmett laughing almost hysterically. "Don't be ridiculous, Sebastian. Zenia can't attend. It would be career-suicide. You won't be able to pretend to be with Lexy with her around." Putting his hands on his hips again, he jutted his chin out in a gesture of stubbornness. "Besides, they only had the two tickets available, otherwise they've sold out."

"They've sold out?" Seb didn't seem convinced.

"Completely." Emmett nodded flatly. "There's limited seating at these things, Sebastian and we waited until the last minute to accept the invite."

"Well, maybe I simply won't go then?" Seb crisscrossed

his arms over his chest defiantly.

"You're being downright childish now, Sebastian," Emmett barked. "I thought you wanted to go out on a high, retire while the whole nation still loved you? Now, you're telling me you'd throw that all away because I can't arrange for an extra ticket for your current fling?"

"Girlfriend," Seb corrected, a hostility to his voice.

When Emmett bared his teeth in a snarl, Zen stepped between them, raising her hands up—palms out like stop signs.

"Guys. Cool it," she ordered. "I don't have to go. It's fine." She looked at Seb, dropped her hand to hold his, comfortingly. "Maybe next time we'll go together." Then she turned to Emmett, her expression hardening defensively. "I appreciate the fact you're trying to look out for Seb, Emmett, but we cannot keep up this farce forever. At some point, we'll come clean and that can either be with your knowledge and planning or without it. It's your choice. Just know it's coming and likely soon."

Emmett's grimace deepened, but he nodded in acknowledgement. "One more week, that's all I ask." His gaze drifted back to Seb. "You know I have your best interest at heart, buddy. I do. I'm trying my best to look out for you."

As his scowl softened, Sebastian's tense posture eased. "Give us a little time, Emmett. I'll meet you back at the house later."

As his agent bowed his head, reluctantly retreating back toward the exit, the door flew open, no knock, no announcement. Lexy burst in, waltzing inside as though floating atop a cloud, her super wide grin at risk of splitting her pretty pink lips at the crease.

"Do you know?" She screeched in excitement; her attention focused in on Zen. "Has he told you? Oh my God, Zenia. He's invited me to a charity gala on Saturday night. I'll get dressed up, ballgown and all, and mingle with the rich and famous. It's a dream come true!"

As her sister bounced around, her feet treating the floor like a trampoline while she whooped her utter exhilaration, Zen felt a heaviness weigh in her gut, a trepidation swirling there, rising bile to the back of her throat. She might have tried to be the bigger person, to not mind missing out, but jealously clawed at her core, reminding her once again of the lies and deceit that still festered within her and Seb's special relationship. She longed to be free of it, to be with him as his partner and to not have to tell anymore painful, soul-eating lies.

In a way, a part of her was happy for her sister, content Lexy was achieving her dreams, but the happiness was double-edged and Zen knew with each success of Lexy's, another shovel of dirt buried the grave of her own relationship with Sebastian. And, if it kept going this way, Zen didn't know if there would be anything left to revive.

CHAPTER 13

The huge comfy-looking bed in the warmly lit room was topped with a heavy navy-patterned duvet and a monstrous assortment of pillows piled high against the timber bedhead and dove-white wall behind. To the right was an adjoining bathroom—small and simple—on the left, a curtained entrance led to a compact second story balcony, while directly opposite, sleekly covered by mirrored sliding doors, was a large clothing closet. Although the room was minimalist in design and decoration, there were still a couple of items inside that alluded to the owner.

Two framed photos—one of the Andino family in a posed embrace and one of Melrose as a puppy—sat atop the wooden nightstand next to a blue lamp and a mystery novel. Above the bed was a beautiful painting of an idyllic seascape and hanging in the center of the curtain rod by the balcony door was a metal windchime decorated with purple dolphins and blue waves. The instrument tinkled in the cool night air, serenading a sweet song of jingling notes, so peaceful in the otherwise silent night.

Curled in the center of the bed, surrounded by chubby mounds of cushion, Zen lounged with Melrose, her beloved canine's head in her lap as she leaned back and stared at the ceiling. It was Saturday night, the evening of the charity gala and her envious thoughts hadn't stopped spinning since Lexy and Seb's attendance was announced on Thursday. While she had no desire to prance and preen around amongst the celebrity crowd—something her sister would likely sell a kidney for—Zen still longed to attend, to be included in something with Seb, to be seen together, to make their relationship public.

When would it finally be her turn to be on his arm? To be special enough to be included publicly in his life? Even the thought of being able to be honest with her own dear family had her heart beating faster, an exhilaration buzzing through her limbs. She cared deeply for Sebastian and was ready for the whole world to know, but now she had to wait another week, suffer through another seven days of lies and secrets. And, even after all that, there was no certainty. Emmett could once again convince Seb to hold out a little longer, another week, then two—would it ever end?

She released another wounded sigh and heard the rumble of Mel's mimic as it vibrated across her thigh. Even with all the wonderful things happening for the opening week of her business, she'd spent all day today and all day yesterday feeling sad and sorry for herself and now she'd passed that depression onto her dog. It was a very solemn situation indeed. She gazed down at him and scratched his head.

"You're a good boy, Mel," she told him.

He raised his head to look at her, his mouth opening, smiling as he panted.

As she bent to place a kiss on his nose, a thunderous clomping of footsteps drew their attention to the open bedroom door in time to see Lexy blunder inside, two different high heels on her feet and her sapphire gown hanging loose and unzipped around her shoulders.

"I need help," she whined as she hobbled in front of

the mirrored closet doors and looked at her reflection. "Seb will be here in a few minutes."

Zen lifted Mel's head from her lap and climbed off the bed to go stand by her sister. The contrast between their looks and outfits was quite startling. While Lexy was all dolled-up, gorgeous and immaculate with her perfect hairstyle, makeup and dazzling dress, Zen was barefaced, her hair in a tousled bun, wearing grey sweatpants and a violet hoodie. With Lexy donning heels, uneven as they were, Zen's bare feet had her standing even shorter beside her sister than usual. Tearing her gaze from the mirror, Zen ignored the ache weighing in her chest, dragging her mood even lower and gave her sister her full concentration.

"You look stunning, Lexy," she told her reassuringly. "That dress is perfect. The color really suits you."

"I know." Lexy huffed and waved a hand at her shoes. "I'm going to wow the crowd tonight, but I need to pick the right heels." She turned her ankle this way and that giving Zen a good view as she watched herself in the mirror and then switched feet, doing the same with the other. "Zen, I need help. Which ones?"

Zen admired both the moonlight-silver colored shoes, but couldn't see much difference in either besides the fact that one was slightly chunkier and had a higher heel. She let her sister twist her ankles at her again, further considering the similar options and then pointed at her preference.

"I'd go with the shorter, more delicately strapped ones. They're probably more suited to the formal occasion."

Lexy stepped that foot forward, looked at it from all angles and then nodded her agreement. "This is why God made sisters."

"Why?" Zen scoffed out her amusement. "To be your fashion stylist?"

Lexy giggled. "No, because you always know what I want, sometimes before I even know it myself."

Zen quirked a dark eyebrow. "Really?"

Again, Lexy nodded. "Just look at Sebastian."

"What about Sebastian?" Zen's heart dropped to her stomach and she felt like she was going to be sick.

"You told me I'd have to work hard to achieve my stardom and that I couldn't claim celebrity status by relying on my association with him."

Relief had Zen relaxing her clenched jaw, but she gave her sister a look of puzzlement. "That's not exactly what I said, Lex."

"But, that's exactly what I plan on doing tonight, Zen," Lexy boasted. "Now that I have the opportunity, I'm going to schmooze up to everyone and anyone of importance at the gala and really earn my time in the spotlight." Her bold grin sparkled in the warm light of the bedroom, glittering like the jewelry draped around her neck and dangling from her ears.

"I'm not sure that's quite the same concept as *working hard*," Zen told her. "That's more like using your gift of the gab to play the room and win people over."

Lexy shrugged. "It's hard, and takes time and energy, so it's like the same thing."

Zen tilted her head and frowned. "Is it though?"

"Anyway, it's worth the effort. Emmett told me that while Seb's still hot at the moment, he's on the outs, so I have to get in and make my mark now while I still can."

Zen crossed her arms over her chest. "Did he now?"

"Yeah. He told me Seb had the ability to be really big, have real international superstardom—you know—but, that he makes poor choices that pull him down."

"Right." Zen gritted her teeth tightly against the desire to say something nasty about Seb's agent and took a deep, calming breath. "Did he tell you what those poor choices were?"

Lexy shook her head. "Nope. Just that Seb's changed and doesn't trust his agent anymore. Emmett told me you should always trust your agent." She said it with such earnest resolve as though mentally judging Seb for not respecting this fact.

"Of course, he did."

Emmett was bound to be critical knowing Seb no longer valued his opinion as he once had, but the agent was in turn letting down his own client by not listening to his new wants and goals. While it was obvious Emmett cared for Seb and believed he was trying to do right by his long-term friend, his failure to listen and understand was affecting their relationship with each other and had the ability to destroy it forever. Zen might not have liked the man, but she didn't want Seb to lose his pseudo-brother.

When Zen pulled herself free of her thoughts, she noticed Lexy staring at her, assessing her expression.

"You know that I don't like him like that, Zen?" Her sister's voice was sincere, compassionate as she laid a hand on Zenia's shoulder. "The whole relationship thing is only a front for the media. Emmett thinks it will help us both secure a bigger fan base, that's all. Seriously. I thought you should know, you know?"

Zen dropped her arms from her chest, easing her rigid posture. "I thought as much, Lex. It's okay."

Lexy gave her a half-hearted laugh and turned back to the mirror, taking in her reflection once more. "It's only—I know you like him. I'm freeing the road as it were. He's all yours."

"Uh—thanks?" Zen gaped, her mouth opening and closing as she searched for an appropriate answer, but the tooting of a car horn outside cut her off before she could decide on something suitable.

As Mel barked and leapt off the bed and out of the room, Lexy hobbled to the balcony in her uneven shoes and peered down below.

"He's here," she exclaimed and hitched up the hem of her dress. "Could you be a doll and greet him? I'll only be another minute or two." With that she lumbered awkwardly out the room and across the hall.

Releasing a pained sigh, Zen did as her sister instructed, descending the staircase and walking to the front door as a knock pounded on the wooden frame. Mel's nose was pressed to the door, waiting eagerly to greet the welcome visitor, but she directed him back and told him to sit. Obediently, he obeyed, but it didn't stop his furry tail from waggling with a thump, thump, thump on the polished floorboards.

After a moment's hesitation, resting her hand on the doorknob, she opened it and greeted Seb with a small smile. "Hi," she said as Mel darted forward. "Stay," she ordered, worried his fluffy hide might soil Seb's attire.

Once more, the pooch complied, but this time he showed his misery by collapsing flat to the floor, his droopy chops hung in a gloomy frown.

"Hello," Seb crooned delightedly, inching swiftly forward before noticing the sad canine face behind Zen. "Aw, sorry, boy," he apologized to Mel. "But it's best if you stay there tonight. I'll give you pats next time."

When Seb's captivating dark eyes met hers again, Zen felt her heart lurch, desire heating her blood. He looked so smolderingly sexy in his tuxedo, so movie star good-looking that she had to look away or risk kissing him right there on the spot.

"Lex will be down in a minute," she informed him, poking a thumb behind her. "She's adding the finishing touches to her outfit."

"I missed you today," Seb confessed quietly, his bulky form looming closer to her. "I hoped you might have been around for the learn-to-swim class, but Amy told me you had piles of paperwork to get through."

"I'd been putting it off." She shrugged and still couldn't quite meet his eyes again. "I thought today was a good day to stop procrastinating."

"So, you chose to avoid me instead?"

Her gaze flicked to his, searching his eyes. "I didn't avoid you."

"No. You simply made yourself busy, so you were too distracted to see me." He leaned against the doorframe, his arms crossed, and a cheeky smile playing on his lips.

Zen lifted her chin, finally holding his gaze again, a challenge in her stare. "Can you blame me, Sebastian? I'm so tired of all the falsities and secrets. I just want to be with you. I want us to be able to go out in public together. The gala tonight, you going with Lexy, having people continue to think you're a couple as my feelings for you grow, it's hurting my heart." She laid a hand there and shook her head, eyes stinging with hot welling tears. "I'm starting to think I won't last another week." Her voice caught and she swallowed, the tears falling down her cheeks as she blinked tightly.

As she quickly wiped at her face, Zen felt Seb's soft fingertips brush dampness from her skin. She looked up at him, up into the concern in his eyes, the fear there and took a sharp breath as he lowered his face closer to hers.

"I'm so sorry," he told her. "I never meant to put you in this situation." He touched his nose to hers, his mouth tickling her lips.

"Okay, I'm ready." It was a gloriously loud and proud announcement from the bowels of the house.

Zen jumped away from Seb, out of his grasp, wiping quickly at her eyes again, before turning to see her sister skipping keenly down the staircase.

"Let's get this sexy ass on the road." Lexy wiggled her hips and appeared unaware of the intimate moment she'd interrupted as she approached them. Passing Zen, she grabbed Seb by the arm, dragging him back outside before waving a hand in the air. "Don't wait up, Zen. I plan to make this a late one."

"Wait, I was—" Seb blurted, but was yanked around and pulled down the front stairs before he could continue.

At the waiting limousine, he stole a glance over his shoulder, a look of bewilderment on his face before Lexy pushed him inside. After her sister waggled her fingers in a final goodbye, Zen inhaled a shaky breath and shut the front door, her heart a little more broken.

CHAPTER 14

Ruby and emerald silk banners scooped along the ceiling of the Brisbane Marriot's Grand Ballroom, spreading out like the petals of an exotic flower from the chandelier at the center. The same colors of the South-East Athletes Charity Gala decorated table centerpieces in floral displays and alternated as chair ribbons from table to table. A raised black stage with microphone and large, boxy speakers at each end sat at the front of the room by the darkened windows which offered an incredible view of the city lights beyond. The roar of zealous conversation and joyous laughter hummed through the multitude of fancily dressed guests. Champagne-filled glasses sparkled on spinning silver trays as waitstaff twirled this way and that, in constant motion, serving, collecting, refreshing.

When Sebastian and Lexy entered, arm in arm, the look of awe on the young social media influencer's face was utterly priceless. It was as though all her Christmases had come and she didn't know which presents to open first.

"Oh my God," she exclaimed. "That's"—she pointed to someone in the distance, before quickly pointing to someone else—"And that's…" She lost her words, her breath and ended up gasping, covering her mouth in complete shock.

"I take it you know everyone then?" Seb teased, giving her a small smile.

Lexy nodded, her eyes still dish-like in size as she stared around the room fascinated.

While Seb was pleased to make someone's dreams come true, he couldn't stop thinking about his own and the gorgeous woman he'd left behind. It pained his own heart seeing Zen so distraught, struggling so deeply with keeping their budding relationship a secret. He, too, found it exhausting having to maintain the farce every time he ran into a fan or was accosted by the media. He longed to have their relationship out in the open, to allow them the freedom to explore their special bond and where it might lead them. He had a deep hope that it could become something more permanent and lasting, that maybe their connection could lead to that wonderful partnership, that extraordinary union he'd only dreamed of.

Thinking of it brought a flashback of Zenia's grave expression, of the agony in her eyes when he'd stared into them, standing before her at the front door. It stabbed at his chest, how all these lies had turned such a vibrant, exuberant woman into a shell of her former self. Even more than that, it hurt him that he knew how easy it was to fix, and he could remove her misery in an instant. It was a simple decision, something he had complete power over and yet he was letting the woman he was falling in love with suffer just to keep his career thriving. Was it worth it? Had it ever been?

Lexy slipped her arm free of his and gestured out toward the famous crowd. "I'm going to mingle," she told him excitedly. "I'll meet you at our table a little later."

As Seb nodded his agreement, she'd already disappeared, wading through glamorously outfitted stars and tuxedoed sportsman.

"I'm glad to see you didn't fight me on attendance."

The familiar satisfied tones of Emmett's voice had Seb

glancing to his side as his agent and old friend approached. In a tuxedo of his own, his hair slicked neatly in place, Emmett greeted him with a glistening grin, a little too smug for Seb's liking.

"You look surprised to see me," his agent told him. "I thought you'd be glad of the company, especially seeing your date has already ditched you."

Seb narrowed his gaze and licked his lips, trying to settle the fury firing through his veins. "I guess I'm a little surprised at how you managed to get a ticket, Emmett. Didn't you tell Zen and me they were all sold out?"

Emmett rolled his eyes and took a sip of his champagne. "Oh, a ticket became available. They do sometimes."

Seb balled his hands into fists, but held them tightly at his side. "It didn't occur to you to offer the ticket to Zen instead, especially considering the situation and all."

Emmett looked at him as though that idea was the most absurd thing he'd ever heard. "You can't be serious, Sebastian? I told you it was a terrible idea for Zenia to come. She would have ruined everything we've got going with Lexy at the moment. Once we get through this next week, we can assess our options and then see what we can do with her." He took another sip and looked out over the crowd, his smile still gaudy and wide.

"*Do with her?*" Seb spat angrily. "Zen is not an extra on a movie set, Emmett. She's a woman I care very deeply for. You should show her more consideration than that."

"Oh, please," his agent tsked. "You're not in love with her, Seb. It's all happened too quickly. You haven't had time to really get to know her. You're in love with her lifestyle, that boring little town, probably, but not her."

Seb staggered back a step as though he'd suffered a physical blow, but it was a sudden realization that had him losing his footing, not the toxic bite of Emmett's words.

"What?" He breathed the word, more to himself than to his old friend.

"Sorry, buddy. I didn't mean to hurt you," Emmett told him, slapping a hand to his shoulder in support. "I had to tell you the truth. You need to snap out of this fantasy, stop making bad decisions and focus back on your career and your future."

"No." Seb shook his head, clearing his thoughts as he brushed off Emmett's hand. "No. Not that. You said I'm in love with her."

"No. I said you're *not* in love with her," Emmett corrected.

Seb's heart skipped a beat and he felt like his feet were floating above the ground. "No, but I think I am, Emmett. I think I've fallen for her." He grabbed his agent by the shoulders and pulled him into a tight, brief hug. "Thanks, buddy. I needed to hear that."

He released Emmett as abruptly as he'd embraced him, making his agent stumble backward as he tried not to spill his champagne.

"What? Sebastian, what are you talking about?" Emmett covered the top of his glass, stopping the swaying liquid from escaping as he glared in total confusion at his client.

But Seb had already begun backing away. "Look after Lexy, will you?" He asked, but didn't wait for a response.

As Seb ran out the main doors and back into the elevator lobby, Emmett called after him.

"It's only been a week, Sebastian. No one falls in love in a week."

But, what Seb knew now and what Emmett still didn't understand was that love blossomed differently in everyone and was never restricted to a timeframe of any kind.

CHAPTER 15

In the darkened living room, with curtains drawn to the outside streetlights and the ongoing night, the widescreen television flashed, illuminating the cream walls in glowing colors and dancing shadows. A tense soundtrack of instrumental music built suspense, seeming louder and more foreboding in the quiet peace of the near vacant space. Scraps of popcorn littered the inside of a large bowl seated on top of the central coffee table next to an empty wine glass and a fitness magazine. Against the far wall, curled up in the fetal position on the floral-patterned sofa was Zenia, her head resting on the couch's cushy arm, her attention focused intently on the scenes unfolding. Melrose was snuggled at her feet on the other side of the sofa, head resting on her heels as he snored softly, eyes closed and tongue hanging loose.

Having been unable to face a romantic comedy or any kind of soppy love-story movie after what had transpired earlier, Zenia had switched channels to a chilling thriller and enjoyed the easy distraction. She was almost ready for bed, prepared to put the horrible day behind her and start anew tomorrow, trying once more to keep up the façade Emmett had created, hoping it wouldn't grow more and more difficult as each day passed. But she'd decided to wait a little longer before retiring upstairs, just another few minutes. Perhaps Lexy would be uninterested by the prestigious event and come home early? Perhaps she wouldn't even be let in? Or maybe Seb would tell everyone the truth about their faked relationship and announce his fondness for her instead?

Zen shook her head slightly, knowing how ludicrous that thought was. Though, the action still didn't stop her from hoping. It upset her to think that her sister and Seb were having a good time together, laughing and embracing, their friendship growing, maybe even giving life to the lie they'd been telling.

Jealously constricted Zen's chest and she hugged her arms tighter against her body. She couldn't think too deeply about it. She had to focus on the movie.

Look, the killer's back. What's he doing now? She led her thoughts along a new tangent in an effort to dull the pain.

Suddenly, there was a knock at the door on screen and an echo filled the house. Mel snorted and roused, his head lifting, eyes zooming in on the front door as Zen glanced around trying to distinguish if the noise was from the television or somewhere else. Then it happened again—the rhythmic tap, tap, tap—and this time Zen was certain it was coming from her own front entrance.

With a bark, Mel leapt off the sofa and hurried toward it. Forcing herself free of the tight ball she'd curled into, Zen followed suit, shuffling slowly after him. While it wasn't late, it wasn't exactly a decent time to call either, so Zen couldn't imagine who the visitor might be. Covering a yawn with the back of her hand, she unlocked the door and pulled it warily inward.

"Yes," she said, cautiously assessing the appearance of her late-night caller. When she realized their identity, still all formally attired in his black and white tuxedo, her knees weakened and her eyes widened in shock.

"Zenia," Seb stepped across the threshold and greeted

Mel with a few strokes to the head. "I know it's late. I hope you don't mind me coming in."

When he walked further inside, she automatically shut the door, her mind still stunned and reeling from his surprise arrival.

"What are you doing here, Seb?" With the door closed, she leaned against it, using its solid sturdiness to keep upright. "Aren't you supposed to be at the gala with Lexy?"

Mel circled around Seb's legs a couple of times, obviously so pleased with the visitor and with the warm greeting he'd received before flopping on the ground beside him.

"Well, yes," Seb agreed, bending to rub Mel's silky ear again. "And, no." He straightened and strode back toward her. "I know I'd planned to go to the gala and I did—I even made it inside—but when I saw Emmett there—"

"Emmett?" She cut him off and crossed her arms. "I thought he told us he couldn't get extra tickets?"

"He lied. He does that sometimes when he's being overprotective or when he thinks he knows what's best for me."

"Or when he's trying to keep you away from women he doesn't approve of?" Zen offered.

"You might be right," he told her, a smirk pinching his lips. "But, none of that matters. Not now." He grabbed her hands, freed them from their tight hold around her chest and then held them warmly in his. "I came here tonight to tell you something, Zen. Something really important and something I should have had the guts to tell you earlier." He pulled her closer to him and raised her hands to his lips, kissing the back of them as he gazed down at her in adoration. "I know it's only been a week, that we still have so much more to learn about each other, but it's been one of the best weeks of my life, Zen. Being in this beautiful town, doing good work, helping to inspire such a wonderful community, and most of all getting to spend time with you, discovering what an amazing person you are, how passionate and driven, how caring and absolutely gorgeous you are—all of it has made me feel rejuvenated, like a better person. It's what I want, Zen, what I see in my future, it's what I'm back here fighting for."

Zen struggled for breath as Seb slipped her hands around the nape of his neck and moved his own to her waist. She felt overwhelmed and excited and terrified and ecstatic all at once, and her heart couldn't decide whether to thump out a samba rhythm or miss a few beats.

"I'm sorry I've been such a fool and it's taken me so long to realize how much you've changed my world, but I finally have, and what I know now, Zenia, is that it's you. I'm falling in love with you. I think it hit me the moment I saw you all tangled up in that red ribbon. It was as though you were giftwrapped just for me, like destiny had intervened and presented you to me. You might think it's crazy, our relationship is so new, but I know how I feel, how much I care for you, Zen and I don't want to hide it anymore. I'm falling in love with you, I want to be with you and I'm not afraid to tell the whole world."

She was breathless and flushed, hot tears pooling in her eyes. This was all she'd wanted and so much more. She had needed them to be honest, no more secrets, no more sneaking around. She'd longed to be able to walk along the beach, hand-in-hand, with the man she thought of as her loving boyfriend, but this—it was so much more than she'd ever expected. Sebastian DuMont—superstar celebrity athlete and kind-hearted, affectionate man of her dreams—was actually falling in love with her. He had chosen her over improving his fan base, chosen her over Lexy and Emmett and their fame-focused motives, and chosen her—an ordinary, small-town girl, with no desire to be in the spotlight—as the woman he could see a future with. It was mind-blowing, life-altering and she couldn't have wished for anything better.

Zen's whole body tingled. A mix of jubilant emotions burst like fireworks within her, making her feel weightless and deliriously happy. As warm tears trickled down her flushed cheeks, she opened her mouth to answer him, but her breath caught on a choked sob, her elation and relief exhibiting in sudden, uncontrollable weeping.

Seb smiled at her, a soft chuckle escaping his lips as he wiped at her face, smoothing the moisture away. "Those better be happy tears," he told her cheerfully.

She nodded enthusiastically, her voice still choked, muted with so much sentiment and excitement. Then she pulled him against her, his strong body against the curves of hers and pressed her mouth to his, her fervent kiss so sincere and tender, saying everything he needed to know and more.

CHAPTER 16

As laughter boomed through the large kitchen from the adjacent dining area, the hot fragrance of spicy cinnamon, roasted almond and juicy apple sailed free of the warm oven when it opened to reveal the baked desert. Another Monday night, another Andino family dinner, but this time they were down one daughter and once again joined by a special guest. While Gabriella dished out portions of the apple-almond pie, Leo, Sebastian and Zenia remained seated around the timber dining table discussing the events of the past weekend.

After admiring the man she loved referring to as her boyfriend and cuddling closer to him, her hand in his, Zen looked at her father and shook her head. "I can't believe you knew."

"He only guessed." Gabriella clarified as she took her seat beside her husband. "Your father, he watched you both at the last dinner and told me he saw the chemistry. He knew then that Lexy wasn't a part of the picture."

"So, you let me lie to you?" Zen gawped, amused by the realization.

"Not lie," Leo amended. "You simply protected the truth until you were both ready for it to be revealed."

"How very diplomatic of you, Leo." Seb praised. "I'm pleased our deception didn't upset you and Gabriella too much. Had I been honest with myself and Zen from the beginning, I could have saved us a lot of effort and heartache."

"Yes," Gabriella nodded, "but sometimes you have to go through the hard times to understand and appreciate the good."

Seb gazed affectionately at Zen and brushed his lips briefly, sweetly to hers. "That's very true. Very true." He rubbed his nose against Zen's and hugged her even closer to his side.

When Zen looked back at her parents, their satisfied smiles said it all.

"Go. Eat." Gabriella gestured to the desserts in front of them, waving a hand to the cream and ice-cream additional options around the table. She watched carefully as Seb took his first bite and almost burst in anticipation of his reaction. "You like it?" She asked him eagerly.

Seb released a little moan of pleasure and then winked at her. "Delicious, Gabriella. Just as you promised."

Zen's mother looked proud and content as she took her own first bite. After swallowing, she questioned them. "So, tell us this news of Lexy's?"

"I thought she might have told you, Mum." Zen looked at Seb and then her father.

"We only know she has gone to Sydney with Sebastian's agent," Leo explained. "She said it was a big opportunity."

"Yes, it is." Seb nodded. "Emmett's offered to represent her. She networked well at the South-East Athletes Charity Gala on Saturday night and made such a good impression on a couple of the bigwigs in the media industry. One of them offered her a sportwear modeling spot in a national magazine, which will see her image boosted and send more industry jobs her way. The other has quickly become her new romantic interest, much to the excitement of the tabloids. When Emmett found out about the connections, he jumped at the chance to represent her."

"Probably because he knew he was about to lose his best client," Zen added.

She was pretty sure Emmett had decided to compromise and cut his loses once he knew for certain he wouldn't be getting Seb to renew his contract with the Icon Agency. Adding Lexy to his client list, especially considering her rapid rise on the celebrity ladder, was the next best thing and softened the blow of losing his biggest client.

Seb smirked at her. "He has been supportive of Lexy from the beginning." His grin was reassuring as he turned his attention back to the older Andinos. "Emmett must really see potential in her, especially to want to bring her back to Sydney and introduce her to the management team. You should be very proud of her."

"Oh, we are. We are." Gabriella gushed. "We are very proud of both our daughters." She gazed devotedly at Zen. "You have always surpassed all our expectations, my gorgeous Zenia. We have always been very proud of all you've accomplished." She slid an arm across the table and grasped her daughter's hand in hers.

"And now with Lexy following her dreams," Leo interjected, "we heard you might be taking a new business partner on board."

"Oh, really, Dad?" Zen teased. "What gossip vine did you hear that from? Amy, maybe?"

Leo's salt and pepper moustache twitched as he tried for an innocent expression.

"Seb would be a wonderful addition, Zenia." Gabriella nodded her approval. "There's no need to be coy about it."

"I'm not being coy, Mum. It's just a bit early. We've only started discussing it." She looked to Seb for support and he chuckled at her.

"All you have to know right now, Leo, Gabriella"—he looked to each of them—"is that I'm crazy about your wonderful daughter, I'm committed to staying in town and that I plan on spending as much time with Zen as possible. From there, we'll see what happens. We've discussed plans for a swim school, for a competitive swimming club maybe, something that would be good for both Poseidon's Shore Health Club and the local community."

"How lovely." There was a satisfied sparkle in Gabriella's eyes again as she gazed from Seb to her daughter. "Our Zenia has always shared your passion for the water."

Zen's cheeks blushed under her parents' stare, but her heart was light, her chest uplifting with a contentment and bliss she'd never experienced before. It was amazing to hear Seb announce his feelings and what their plans for the future entailed. It was even more incredible to know that they had shared plans for the future. As a teenager sitting in her bedroom dreaming of all she could achieve and crushing on a certain swimming superstar, she'd never imagined that this would have become her reality. She was exceptionally grateful and knew that as each day passed, their special relationship was becoming deeper, more cemented and lasting, and Seb was quickly becoming the love of her life.

"So, you say you're crazy for our Zenia, Sebastian?" Leo posed curiously. "Does that mean an engagement may be around the corner?"

When Seb gaped and then laughed, Zenia scolded her father. "Dad."

"Oh, and marriage and babies?" Gabriella clucked with delight.

"Mum." Zenia slapped a hand over her face, her cheeks now on fire with embarrassment.

"No. No." Seb laughed again and pulled her hand away so he could stare into her eyes. "It's a good question, Zen. I'm glad they asked." He shot a kind smile at Leo and

Gabriella and then focused in on Zen, shifting so he was facing her. "I know we're at the start of our journey, Zenia, that we really don't know what's around the corner for us, but I want you to know that I'm committed to a future with you, that I feel at home when I'm with you and I'm completely in love with you. Whatever happens now, I know we will embrace it together, and love and support each other always. You're my dream girl, Zen. It's me who should've had your poster up on my wall."

As Gabriella cooed with pleasure and Leo chuckled in approval, Seb bent his head and placed a tender kiss to Zen's lips. She clutched him closer, enjoying feeling the solidness of his body against hers and knew exactly what he'd meant when he said he felt at home with her. Zen felt it, too, their special chemistry, their innate bond, the feeling that they might just be meant-to-be. It made it all the more remarkable that they'd found each other, chosen one another and decided to share a promising future together. Their two worlds might have collided—his one of celebrity and fame, hers one of simple pleasures and hard work—but through it all they'd discovered the perfect loving partner and a life they'd always dreamed of.

THE END

CHECK OUT THESE BOOKS BY TAMMY MANNERSLY

The new doctor in town is attracting some attention, especially of the female persuasion, but art teacher, Erica Townsend is blissfully unaware until she ends up injured and in his office. Too bad she'd vowed to resist love—that traitorous emotion, the destroyer of lives—after numerous failed relationships. Something about Matt, about their electrifying connection has her wondering if he might just be...*the one.*

Dr. Matthew Garrick is tired of playing wing-man for his best friend. It isn't that he wishes to look for love, rather the opposite. But the eagerness of some of the single women in their small country town unnerves him. That is, until a certain stunning brunette appears in the waiting room of his medical practice. Her touch sparks something deep inside him, jolting his heart into a new rhythm and Matt makes it his mission to win's Erica love. Can he convince her to take a risk on him and what they share together?

As the good doctor strives to show Erica that love doesn't have to come at a price, his dangerous secret admirer threatens to prove otherwise.

Whoever said love wasn't dangerous?

You can't hide from destiny….

Callum Hawthorne is one of those lucky guys who seem to have it all. He's a wealthy property tycoon, the CEO of his family's company. He's handsome, intelligent and charming and has a gorgeous new woman on his arm every week. But there's one thing still missing – the love of his life, Lucy Spencer.

Fourteen long years ago, Lucy left for college and cut off all contact with Cal, leaving their mutual friend

Madison as his only connection. That was until in his effort to save his deceased father's beloved Gold Coast property, The Calypso, Cal contacts Insight Marketing, the best advertising firm in Melbourne, and discovers his Lucy among the team.

Successful marketing executive, Lucy Spencer had managed to avoid her ex-best friend for nearly half their lives. Fearful of trusting him, loving him and having her heart broken all over again, Lucy tries to keep her distance from him, but discovers that there is a fine line between love and hate, and maybe – just maybe – Cal could be her inescapable destiny.

~Persuading Lucy was a 1st Place WINNER for the prestigious Chatelaine Book Awards for Romance Fiction and will quickly become your new favourite read.

Invited by one brother, tempted by the other...

Former Australian playboy Blake Davenport knows his billionaire brother, David, is capable of anything to ensure he gets what he wants. But manipulating his young daughter's beautiful teacher into marriage is unacceptable.

Gwen Deveraux is grateful for the invitation to spend Christmas and New Year's with her beloved student's family, especially when her handsome host is so eager for her company. After surviving a broken heart, she is finally ready to give love another chance.

But, who with?

The illustrious David Davenport whose real motives seem hidden behind charm? Or his roguish brother, Blake, who has tempted her heart and body from the very moment they met?

NOW AVAILABLE IN EBOOK AND PRINT AT ALL MAJOR BOOK RETAILERS.

ABOUT THE AUTHOR

Tammy Mannersly is an Australian author based in Brisbane, Queensland. She loves writing romance, has a fondness for animals, is crazy about movies and enjoys a great Happily Ever After. Her passion for writing started from a very young age and led her to complete a Bachelor Degree in Creative Industries majoring in Creative Writing at Queensland University of Technology. Her novel, *Persuading Lucy*, was a 1st Place WINNER in the 2018 Chatelaine Books Awards for Romantic Fiction, a Chanticleer International Book Awards competition.

You can find out more information about Tammy and her work on her website: www.tammymannersly.com or by visiting:

Facebook:
https://www.facebook.com/tammymannersly

Goodreads:
https://www.goodreads.com/author/show/16935790.Ta
mmy_Mannersly

Instagram:
https://www.instagram.com/tammymannersly/

Twitter: https://twitter.com/TammyMannersly

BookBub: https://www.bookbub.com/profile/tammy-mannersly